Blue Line 5

Vokabeltraining aktiv

Herausgeber: Dr. Frank Haß

Ernst Klett Verlag
Stuttgart • Leipzig

Liebe Schülerinnen und Schüler,

mit *Vokabeltraining aktiv* kannst du alle neuen Vokabeln aus *Blue Line* 5 üben.

Auf jeder Seite findest du einen Kasten mit dem Titel „What's the word?“, wo du die Lücken vervollständigen kannst.

What's the word?

1. Wir werden Australien erkunden. We're going to explore ______ Australia.
2.  My favourite animal is the kangaroo ______.

Sieh dir die Beispiele im Kasten an. Hier musst du z. B.

- den englischen Begriff für das Bild einsetzen
- den deutschen Satz links übersetzen und hierfür das unterstrichene Wort auf Englisch einsetzen.

Wir haben uns auch viele Rätsel und spannende Übungen für dich ausgedacht. Diese findest du immer auf der unteren Hälfte jeder Seite.

Unter der Überschrift *Blue words* findest du alle blau gedruckten Wörter deines Englischbuchs einer *Unit* zusammengefasst.

Hier sind noch einige Tipps, wie du die neuen Vokabeln aus *Blue Line* 5 mit *Vokabeltraining aktiv* üben kannst:

- Vervollständige die Lücken mit Bleistift, so kannst du dich jederzeit korrigieren.
- Deine Lösungen kannst du im Lösungsheft selbst überprüfen.
- Achte immer auf die korrekte Schreibung der Wörter.
- Notiere die Wörter, bei denen du Schwierigkeiten hattest, und lerne sie besonders sorgfältig, z. B. mit Karteikarten. Versuche später noch einmal, die Sätze zu vervollständigen.
- Wenn du alle wichtigen Wörter einer Seite gut gelernt hast, kannst du versuchen, die englischen Übungssätze abzudecken und die deutschen still zu übersetzen.

Nun wünschen wir dir viel Spaß und Erfolg mit *Vokabeltraining aktiv*!

Dein *Blue Line*-Team

What's the word?

1. Meine Damen und Herren, ich werde Sie auf eine Reise mitnehmen.	____________________, I'm going to take you on a trip.
2. Wir werden Australien erkunden.	We're going to ____________ Australia.
3. Das ist ein toller Kontinent.	It's a great ____________.
4. Einst war er Teil der Antarktis.	Once it was part of ____________.
5. Der australische Kontinent ist zwanzig Mal so groß wie Deutschland.	The ____________ continent is twenty times the size of Germany.
6. Die Australier sind sehr lockere Menschen.	Australians are very ____________ people.
7. An der Ostküste gibt es interessante Tiere.	There are interesting animals on the ____________ coast.
8. 	Just think of the ____________.
9. 	My favourite animal is the ____________.

1 Put in the right words.

continent | easy-going | explore | kangaroos | koala | Ladies and gentlemen

1 ____________________, welcome to Australia. People here are very relaxed. Australia is an ____________ country.

2 Together we're going to ____________ the ____________.

3 I'm going to show you some funny animals like the ____________.

4 We're also going to see some ____________, of course.

What's the word?

1. Die meisten Touristen lieben Australien. — ____________ tourists love Australia.
2. Sie mögen die spektakulären Aussichten. — They like the ________________ views.
3. Sie mögen auch all die ungewöhnlichen Tiere. — They also like all the ______________ animals.
4. Die meisten Arten gibt es nur auf diesem Kontinent. — Most ______________ can only be found on this continent.
5. Deshalb ist Australien auch als guter Ort zum Tiere-Beobachten bekannt. — That is why Australia ______________________ a good place to see animals.

2 Find the words. Write them in English and German.

spectacularspeciesunusualmostexplorecontinent

________________________ ________________________

________________________ ________________________

________________________ ________________________

3 Put a circle around the right words.

1. Not everyone likes koalas, but (few • most) people do.
2. She looks strange. Her hair is (nice • unusual).
3. The view is (big • spectacular). Look, the mountain is so huge!
4. There are many unusual (types • species) in Australia.

4 Match the words with the same meaning.

1. special
2. fantastic
3. almost all
4. relaxed
5. go out and have a look

a) spectacular
b) explore
c) unusual
d) most
e) easy-going

What's the word?

1. Die Aborigines leben seit mehr als 50.000 Jahren in Australien.
   The ______________________ have lived in Australia for over 50,000 years.

2. Die Zuwanderung von Europäern nach Australien begann Ende des 18. Jahrhunderts.
   The ______________ of Europeans to Australia started at the end of the 18th century.

3. Als europäische Siedler nach Australien kamen, verloren viele Aborigines die Kontrolle über ihr Land.
   When European settlers came to Australia, many Aboriginal people lost ______________ over their land.

4. 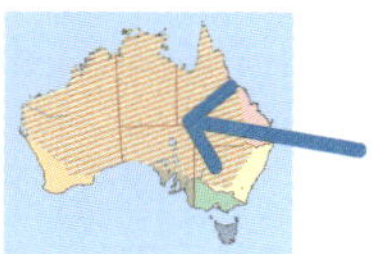
   Aboriginal people used to live in ______________.
   Today most of them live in cities.

5. Manche Aborigine-Kinder gehen aufs Internat.
   Some Aboriginal children go to ______________ ______________.

6. Wenn sie mit der Schule fertig sind, können sie qualifizierte Jobs bekommen.
   When they finish school, they can get ______________ jobs.

7. 
   Some are ______________.

8. Viele Frauen sind Krankenschwestern.
   Many women are ______________.

5 Look at the picture and write the words.

1. ______________________ continent
2. ______________________
3. ______________________
4. ______________________ woman
5. ______________________
6. ______________________

What's the word?

1. Wegen der großen Entfernungen haben die Kinder im Outback Mühe, in die Stadt zu kommen. — Children in the outback ______________ to get to town because of the long distances.
2. Sie können nicht wie andere Kinder die Schule besuchen. — They cannot ______________ school like other children.
3.  — They use a ______________ to watch lessons on TV.
4. Sie treffen ihre Lehrer nur dreimal im Semester. — They only meet their teachers three times a ______________.
5. Sie freuen sich darauf, sie zu sehen. — They ______________ seeing them.

6 Put in the right words.

attend | Australia | boarding school | explore | look forward to | most | nurse | satellite dish | struggle | term | the outback | unusual

E-MAIL

Hi Sam,

Thanks for your e-mail. You wanted to know a bit about my life in ______________. Well, my family and I live in ______________. That's a large area in the centre of Australia. The big cities are far away. That's why I can't ______________ a regular school, and my brothers and sisters can't either. We have a ______________ and watch lessons on the TV instead. That's very cool. But it's not always easy to study at home. Sometimes we ______________ to do all our homework and stay motivated without help from the teachers. My cousin Adina goes to a ______________ in Melbourne. She is hard-working and wants to be a ______________. At the end of the ______________ she usually comes to visit us and we spend ______________ of our time outside. Australia has many ______________ animals. So there's a lot to ______________. I always ______________ seeing Adina because she has so many interesting stories from school to tell. ☺

Love,

Jindalee

What's the word?

1. Man darf nicht respektlos gegenüber der Kultur der Aborigines sein.	You mustn't be ______________ of Aboriginal culture.
2. Es ist nicht akzeptabel, Witze über ihre Kultur zu machen.	It is not ______________ to make jokes about their culture.
3. Es ist nicht in Ordnung, ihre Traditionen zu ignorieren.	It is not OK to ______________ their traditions.
4. Einige Touristen sind echt ignorant. Sie werfen zum Beispiel ihren Abfall auf die Straße.	Some tourists are really ______________. They throw their rubbish on the street, for example.
5. Wir alle sollten mehr Toleranz für das Leben anderer zeigen.	We all should show more ______________ for other people's lives.
6. „Ignorieren" ist ein Verb.	'To ignore' is a ______________.

7 Put a circle around the right words.

1. There are so many English (verbs • species) to learn.
2. Pushing people on the bus is not (acceptable • skilled).
3. People who don't respect other cultures are (easy-going • ignorant).
4. You mustn't be (disrespectful • unusual) when you visit a foreign country.
5. Please don't (ignorant • ignore) me! I would like to talk to you.

8 Make sentences. Put the words in the right order.

1. class • in • is • Shouting • acceptable. • not

____

2. the • test. • I • all • knew • the • verbs • in

____

3. to • survive • Kangaroos • in • water. • the outback • without • struggle

____

4. understand • I • John • don't • is • ignoring • why • me.

____

What's the word?

1. Die meisten Erwachsenen haben zu Hause Höflichkeit gelernt. — Most adults learnt ________________ at home.
2. Ihre Eltern tolerierten keine Unverschämtheit. — Their parents did not tolerate ________________.
3. Meine Oma sagt, dass junge Leute oft Respektlosigkeit zeigen. — My grandma says young people often show ________________.
4. Sie gehört zu einer älteren Generation und war nicht auf der Universität. — She belongs to an older ________________ and did not go to ________________.
5. Junge Menschen haben ihre eigenen Überzeugungen. — Young people have their own ________________.
6. Aber meine Oma denkt, sie sind unhöflich. — But my gandma thinks they are ________________.

9 Look at the pictures and complete the sentences.

1. My grandpa belongs to an older ________________. But he is really cool.
2. When many young people finish school, they go to ________________.
3. I don't like some teenagers' ________________ for the rules.

10 Match the opposites. ↔

1. politeness
2. east
3. term
4. ignore
5. regular

a) west
b) holidays
c) rudeness
d) unusual
e) respect

11 Complete the words.

A A A E E E E E E E E E E I I I I I O O U U

1. b _ l _ _ f
2. _ cc _ pt _ bl _
3. r _ d _
4. _ n _ v _ rs _ ty
5. p _ l _ t _ n _ ss
6. g _ n _ r _ t _ _ n

What's the word?

1. Der Uluru ist ein heiliger Ort für die Aborigines. — Uluru is a __________ place to the Aboriginal people.
2. Vor langer Zeit lebten dort riesige Kreaturen. — Giant __________ lived there a long time ago.
3. Deshalb hat der Uluru eine besondere Bedeutung für die Aborigines. — That is why Uluru has a special __________ to the Aboriginal people.
4. Du kannst den Uluru nur mit einem Reiseleiter besichtigen. — You can only go to Uluru with a __________.
5. Die Reiseleiter werden dich herumführen. — The guides will __________.
6. Sie erlauben kein anstößiges Verhalten. — They don't allow __________ __________.
7. Hier ist die Bewerbung für Besucher. Du musst sie unterschreiben und einschicken. — Here is the __________ for visitors. You have to sign it and __________ it __________.

12 Look at the pictures and complete the sentences.

1. Hi. I'm Sam. I'm your __________. I'll __________ the city.

2. Uluru is a __________ place with a special __________.

3. Welcome to the job. I'm glad your __________ was successful.

4. When you visit Uluru, offensive __________ is not allowed.

5. I'll __________ my application today.

6. Please sign this __________ for visitors.

What's the word?

1. Einige Aborigine-Stämme leben in der Nähe des Uluru. — Some Aboriginal ____________ live near Uluru.
2. Der Uluru ist ein überwältigender Ort. — Uluru is a ____________ place.
3. Jeden Morgen heißen die Stämme die Sonne willkommen. — ____________ morning the tribes welcome the sun.
4.  — Then they take the ____________ to their sacred rock.
5. Man kann bei dieser Tradition zuschauen, aber man muss leise sein und die Regeln respektieren. — You can watch this tradition, but you ____________ be quiet and respect the rules.

13 Put the words in the right group.

boarding school · carpenter · disrespectful · guide · ignorant · kangaroo · nurse · path · rude · term · the outback · university

jobs	nature	behaviour	school and education

14 Put in the right words.

behaviour · beliefs · creatures · disrespectful · ignorant · meaning · need to · sacred · stunning

Many children in Germany are ____________ of their traditions. Their parents don't tell them ____________ stories any more. If you don't know these ____________ stories, it's difficult to understand the ____________ of our traditions. Traditions tell us what good ____________ is. For example, we mustn't be ____________ of other people or ____________ and we ____________ ____________ respect other people's ____________.

What's the word?

1.  My friend used to be a ____________ in Sydney.
2. Dafür brauchte sie keine besonderen Fähigkeiten. — She didn't need any special ____________ for that.
3. Sie hatte keine Berufserfahrung. — She didn't have any ____________.
4. Aber sie ist immer pünktlich. — But she is always ____________.
5. Jetzt arbeitet sie als Reisebürokauffrau. — Now she works as a ____________.
6. Sie ist effizient und fleißig. — She is ____________ and hard-working.
7. Sie bucht normalerweise Reisen, aber manchmal arbeitet sie auch in der Verwaltung oder im Kundendienst. — She usually books holidays, but she sometimes works in the ____________ department or ____________ too.
8. Sie ist froh, dass sie einen unbefristeten Job hat. — She is happy to have a ____________ job.

15 Put a circle around the odd one out and write it in German.

1. nurse • travel agent • bike courier • work experience ____________
2. skilled • administration • punctual • efficient ____________
3. tired • slow • late • punctual ____________

16 Find seven words. (↓ and →) Write them in English and German.

B	I	K	E	C	O	U	R	I	E	R	T
P	Z	U	I	O	P	X	C	A	Q	Y	R
E	I	R	S	K	I	L	L	S	K	L	A
R	B	R	Y	Q	W	E	R	S	F	G	V
M	E	X	A	F	F	I	L	U	C	E	E
A	P	U	N	C	T	U	A	L	R	E	L
N	N	T	P	Y	H	E	S	T	M	B	A
E	H	P	O	T	R	A	L	Z	I	N	G
N	E	F	F	I	C	I	E	N	T	A	E
T	A	P	P	L	I	C	A	T	I	O	N
X	Z	S	H	I	M	S	R	Y	D	F	T

____
____
____
____
____
____
____
____
____
____

What's the word?

1. Ich sah eine Anzeige für einen Elektriker. — I saw an advert for an ______________ .
2. Die Firma sucht einen Muttersprachler. — The company is looking for a ______________ ______________ .
3. Das Gehalt, das sie bieten, ist gut. — The ______________ they ______________ is good.
4. 

— They want to see a ______________ .
5. Sie benötigen auch zwei Referenzschreiben. — They also need two ______________ .
6. Ich rief die Empfangschefin der Firma an. — I phoned the ______________ at the company.
7. Sie sagte mir, ich solle einen Bewerbungsbrief schreiben. — She told me to write a ______________ ______________ .
8. Ich schickte eine E-Mail und schrieb: „Angefügt erhalten Sie meinen Lebenslauf." — I sent an e-mail and wrote 'Please find ______________ my ______________ .'

17 Look at the pictures and complete the sentences.

1. ______________ 2. ______________ 3. ______________

18 Say the words. Then complete the table.

appli**c**ation · **c**ertificate · certifi**c**ate · **C**V · ele**c**trician · electri**c**ian · re**c**eptionist · referen**c**es

sounds like a German 'k'	sounds like a German 'ß'	sounds like a German 'sch'

What's the word?

1. Ich möchte für eine chinesische Firma arbeiten. — I want to work for a ____________ company.
2. Die Firma ist in Hongkong, auf einer Insel nahe der chinesischen Küste. — The company is in Hong Kong on an ____________ near the Chinese coast.
3. Der Job ist im Kundenservice. Also brauche ich gute Kommunikationsfähigkeiten. — The job is in customer service so I need good ____________ skills.
4. Ich schrieb ein Motivationsschreiben und erzählte ihnen von meinen Interessen. — I wrote a ____________ and told them about my ____________.
5. Ich musste Details und die Rechtschreibung beachten. — I had to ____________ detail and to my spelling.
6. Ich schrieb auch einen Bewerbungsbrief. Ich beendete den Brief mit „Mit freundlichen Grüßen“. — I also wrote a letter of application. I ended the letter with '____________'.

19 Complete the dialogue.

attached | certificates | Chinese | efficient | interests | offer | pay attention | personal statement | work experience

1. I've read your CV, but I can't see your ____________.
2. Oh, I thought it was ____________ to the e-mail.
3. Oh, yes. Here it is.
4. I also sent you my school ____________.
5. Good. I can see you're ____________. You also ____________ to detail and have many ____________.
6. Thank you.
7. Your ____________ looks very good. It seems you have a lot to ____________. But do you really want to work in China?
8. Oh, yes. I love ____________ culture! And I speak some Chinese.

What's the word?

1. Der Klimawandel ist für die Welt ein Problem. — ____________ is a problem for the world.
2. Er ist eine große Gefahr für das Great Barrier Reef. — It is a big ____________ to the Great Barrier Reef.
3.  — The ____________ is a very special animal.
4. Die Koralle ist Teil der Unterwasserwelt und sieht aus wie ein Riff aus Stein. — The coral is part of the ____________ world and looks like a ____________ made of stone.
5. Manche Leute sagen, sie sei ein Unterwasserwunder. — Some people say it is an underwater ____________.
6. Sich verändernde Wassertemperaturen sind nicht gut für die Korallen. — ____________ water ____________ are not good for the coral.
7. Veränderungen in der Umwelt verursachen den Tod der Korallen und anderer Unterwasserlebewesen. — Changes in the ____________ cause the ____________ of the coral and other underwater creatures.

20 Match the questions and the answers.

1. Are you worried about the weather?
2. Do you think Tom will be safe?
3. What do you want to do in Australia?
4. What causes the death of the coral?
5. Is there a problem with the reefs?

a) I want to see the underwater reefs.
b) Changes in the environment.
c) Yes, he will. There's no danger.
d) Yes, the changing temperatures are bad for them.
e) No, I'm worried about climate change.

21 Find the words. Write them in English and German.

temperaturewonderdeathreefdangerenvironment

____________ ____________

____________ ____________

____________ ____________

What's the word?

1.  I was on holiday in ____________.

2.  I sat down on the beach and watched the ____________.

3. Ich hörte auch den Geräuschen des großen weiten Meeres zu. – I also listened to the sound of the ____________ open sea.

4. Aber der Strand war voller Vogelexkremente. – But the beach was full of bird ____________.

5. Die Exkremente riechen schlecht und verursachen Schaden an den Bäumen. – The waste smells bad and it causes ____________ to the trees.

6. Die Regierung will das stoppen. – The government wants to ____________ this.

7. Sie haben sich auf ein Programm geeinigt, einige Vögel in den Zoo zu bringen. – They ____________ a ____________ to take some of the birds to a zoo.

8. Ich finde es gut, wenn sich die Menschen für die Umwelt interessieren. – I think it's good when people ____________ the environment.

22 What is it? Write the word.

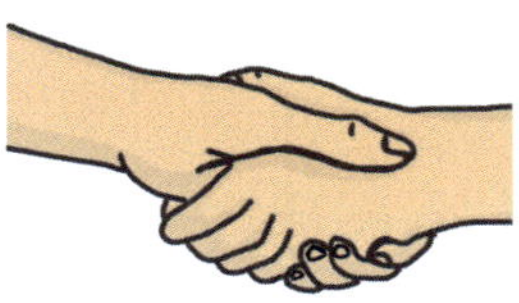   

1. You can see it when it is dark, but it is not a star. ____________
2. It is an island in Italy. ____________
3. things people throw away ____________
4. When you have the same idea, you ____________ an idea.

23 Find the words that rhyme.

belief | care | CV | moon | wide | wonder

1. TV – ____________
2. wear – ____________
3. reef – ____________
4. side – ____________
5. soon – ____________
6. under – ____________

What's the word?

1.  The waste in the oceans is bad for ______________.

2.  It's also a problem for ______________.

3. Walhaie und tropische Fische fressen den Müll und sterben. — ______________ and ______________ fish eat the waste and die.

4. Auch die Delfine und Teufelsrochen sind in Gefahr. — ______________ and ______________ are in danger too.

5. Die Salzwasserkrokodile leben nicht in dieser Gegend und fressen den Müll deshalb nicht. — ______________ don't live in that area so they won't eat the waste.

24 Put the words in the right order.

1. waste • The • from • ship • killed • whale sharks. • the • many

____

2. many • the • Australia • has • manta ray. • interesting • animals • like

____

3. and • live • the • in • Great Barrier Reef. • Turtles • fish • also • tropical

____

25 Right or wrong?

	right	wrong
1. Turtles live in the ocean.	☐	☐
2. The manta ray is a species of fish.	☐	☐
3. Saltwater crocodiles can't survive in the ocean.	☐	☐
4. Waste is a danger for fish and birds.	☐	☐
5. Whale sharks are very small.	☐	☐

What's the word?

1.  ________ often get good jobs.
2. Sie studieren Chemikalien oder Algen. — They study ________ or ________.
3. Wissenschaftliche Jobs ziehen oft Jungen an. — Science jobs often ________ boys.
4. Einige Jungen wollen Physiotherapeuten werden. — Some boys want to become ________.
5. Physiotherapeuten müssen respektvoll und tolerant sein, denn sie arbeiten mit Menschen. — Psychotherapists have to be ________ and ________ because they work with people.
6. Einige Mädchen möchten Klempnerinnen werden. — Some girls want to become ________.
7. Andere möchten als Telefonistinnen für große Firmen arbeiten. — Others want to work as ________ for big companies.
8. Aber ich glaube, niemand möchte in einem Callcenter arbeiten, denn oft zeigen die Leute, die man anruft, keinen Respekt. — But I think nobody wants to work in a ________ because the people you call often don't show ________.

26 Look at the pictures and write the words.

1. ________
2. ________
3. ________

27 Complete the words.

-able -al -ance -ant -ful -ive -ness -ness

1. respect________
2. polite________
3. accept________
4. toler________
5. rude________
6. toler________
7. offens________
8. tropic________

What's the word?

1. Tropische Stürme kommen zur Regenzeit. — Tropical storms come in the ____________.
2. Sie führen zu Problemen für alle. — They ____________ problems for everyone.
3.  — That is why tourists go ____________ during the summer.
4. Dann sind die Schnorchelplattformen sicher. — Then the snorkelling ____________ are safe.
5. Das Ausbleichen durch Sonnenlicht kann ein Problem für die Plattformen sein. — Sun ____________ can be a problem for the platforms.
6. Das Holz erholt sich nicht davon. Es verliert seine Farbe und sieht nicht mehr schön aus. — The wood won't ____________ from it. It loses its colour and doesn't look nice any more.

28 Look at the pictures and complete the sentences.

1. There are many storms in the ____________.

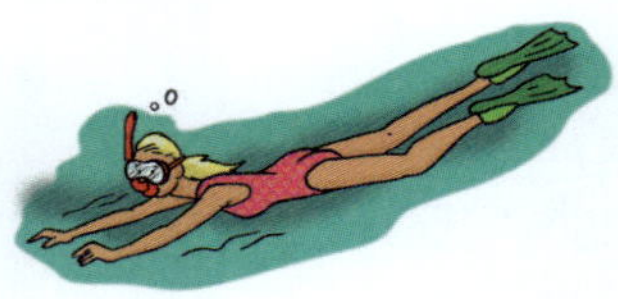

2. She loves ____________.

3. Will the oceans ____________ from all the waste?

29 Put in the right words.

algae | bleaching | chemicals | coral | creatures | danger | rainy season | Reef | results in | snorkelling | will recover

E-MAIL

Hi Dad,

I just visited the Great Barrier ____________ and went ____________.

The ____________ is so beautiful! Coral ____________, however, is a ____________ to the reef. It ____________ the death of the ____________ on the coral. When the algae die, the underwater ____________ lose their food. The ____________ is a problem too because the rain carries ____________ into the ocean. I'm not sure if the sea ____________ from it.

Love,

Liz

What's the word?

1.  ______ are a problem for the environment.
2. Sie können sich bis über hundert Meilen erstrecken. — They can ______ across more than hundred miles.
3. Sie verschmutzen die Ozeane. — They ______ the oceans.
4. Sie sind auch gefährlich für die Schiffe, die vorbeikommen. — They are also dangerous for the ships that ______ .
5. Der Zustand der Strände ist auch schrecklich. — The beaches are in a terrible ______ too.
6. Die Ignoranz der Ölfirmen ist Teil dieses Problems. — The ______ of the oil companies is part of the problem.
7. Es gibt nicht mehr viel Akzeptanz für Ölfirmen. — There's not much ______ for oil companies any more.

30 Put in the right words.

death | oil spills | pollute | recover | species | state | stretch

We hear about ______ almost every month. They often ______ across hundreds of miles. They ______ the water and the beaches and cause the ______ of many underwater ______ and birds. This is not an acceptable ______ for the wildlife. If oil spills happen again and again, the oceans will not ______ from them.

31 Complete the mind map.

algae | chemicals | changing temperatures | coral | coral bleaching | dolphins | more tropical storms | oil spills | death of species | waste | whales

the environment

climate change
______
______
______

other dangers
______
______
______

plants and animals
______ ______
______ ______

What's the word?

1. Viele Leute machen in der Karibik Urlaub. — Many people go on holiday to ______________________.
2. Die sandigen Strände sind sehr beliebt. — The ______________ beaches are very popular.
3. Alle karibischen Inseln haben Hotels. — All ____________________ islands have hotels.
4. Im Herbst kommen wenige Touristen. — Few tourists come in the ________________.
5.  — It is ___________________ season.

1 Look at the pictures and complete the sentences.

1. Many tourists go on holiday to the ________________________ in the winter.
2. The worst time to go is in the ________________ because it is __________________ season.
3. Tourists love the ______________ beaches.

2 Match the words.

1. sandy
2. hurricane
3. autumn
4. Caribbean

a) storms
b) beaches
c) islands
d) season

3 Find the words. Write them in English and German.

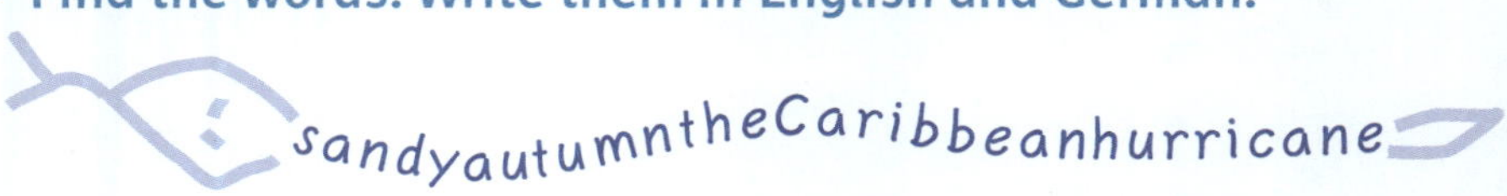

_______________________ _______________________

_______________________ _______________________

What's the word?

1. Die karibischen Inseln waren früher Kolonien.	The Caribbean islands used to be ______________.
2. Manche Inseln waren niederländische Kolonien.	Some islands were ______________ colonies.
3. Andere gehörten den Briten.	Others belonged to ______________.
4. Viele Kariben sind gute Musiker.	Many Caribbean people are good ______________.
5. Sie lieben schnelle Rhythmen.	They love quick ______________.
6. Sie schreiben ihre eigenen Liedtexte.	They write their own ______________.
7. Bob Marley ist ihr Vorbild.	Bob Marley is their ______________.
8. Ihr Ziel ist es, so berühmt zu werden wie er.	Their ______________ is to become famous like him.
9. Zur Zeit gibt es eine Rückkehr von Musik aus den 80ern und 90ern.	There has been a ______________ to music from the '80s and '90s.

4 Look at the pictures and complete the sentences.

1. Jamaica is one of the ______________ islands.

2. Some islands were ______________ colonies.

3. Other islands were Spanish ______________.

4. ______________ came to the Caribbean in the 17th century.

5. Look, the football player is near the ______________!

6. I want to become a famous ______________ one day.

What's the word?

1. Meine Eltern und ich waren in den Ferien auf den Bahamas. — My parents and I went on holiday to ________________.
2. Wir fuhren mit der Fähre dorthin. — We went there by ____________.
3. Die Fähre fuhr ohne Verspätung ab. — The ferry left without ____________.
4. Meine Eltern hatten ein Luxusresort gebucht. — My parents had booked a ________________.
5. Mir gefiel die Unterkunft. — I loved the ________________.
6. Ich werde nie wieder in einer normalen Ferienanlage übernachten. — I will never stay in a regular ____________ again.
7. Meine Schwester mag dennoch lieber Couchsurfing. — But my sister still prefers ________________.

5 Complete the dialogue.

accommodation | the Bahamas | Caribbean | couch surfing | hurricane | luxury resort | musicians | where | why

1 How was your holiday in the ____________?

2 Awesome! We stayed in a ____________ ____________.

3 ____________ was the resort?

4 It was in ____________.

5 What did you like most?

6 I loved the Caribbean ____________. And our hotel was so much better than ____________. But I was afraid to leave our ____________ in the dark.

7 ____________ was that?

8 I thought a ____________ was on its way.

What's the word?

1. Meine Freunde buchten ein Zimmer in einem Hotel in Trinidad. — My friends booked a room at a hotel in ________________.
2. Sie wollten Inselhopping machen. — They wanted to do some island ________________.
3. 

— They took their ________________ with them on the ferry.
4. Sie mussten sie am Gate zeigen. — They had to show them at the ____________.
5. Dann durften sie an Bord der Fähre gehen. — Then they were allowed to ______________ the ferry.
6. Sie liebten die Schönheit der Karibik. — They loved the ______________ of the Caribbean.
7. Sie raubte ihnen den Atem. — It ____________ their ____________________.

6 Choose the right word.

beauty | board | delay | ferry | passport | Trinidad

1. bus • plane • ________________________
2. enter • go in • ________________________
3. Jamaica • Bahamas • ________________
4. early • on time • ________________________
5. gate • ticket • ________________________
6. woman • pretty • ________________________

7 Match the sentence parts.

1. We'll spend our holiday
2. We'll take the ferry
3. We can board
4. But there is a delay
5. I'm glad we can still
6. I'm looking forward

a) because it's cheap.
b) do some island hopping.
c) because of a storm.
d) in Trinidad.
e) to the beauty of the place.
f) at two in the afternoon.

What's the word?

1. Die Britischen Jungferninseln sind für Wassersport berühmt. — ________ are famous for water sports.
2.  — ________ is very popular there.
3. Am Strand gibt es Tauchschulen. — There are ________ on the beach.
4. Man kann unter Wasser Schiffswracks sehen. — You can see ________ under the water.
5. Es ist eine außergewöhnliche Erfahrung. — It is an ________ experience.
6. Unser Hostel bietet auch Tauchstunden an. — Our ________ offers diving lessons too.
7. Sie finden jeden Tag statt. — They ________ every day.

8 Look at the pictures and complete the sentences.

1. The Caribbean is famous for ________.
2. There are many ________ ________ on the islands.
3. Many people go to ________ ________ to go diving.

4. There are many ________ in the Caribbean.
5. Surfing lessons ________ ________ every day.
6. Tourists also want to see the ________.

9 Find the words that rhyme.

delay | ferry | gate | goal | return | sandy

1. learn – ________
2. Mandy – ________
3. pay – ________
4. hole – ________
5. late – ________
6. Jerry – ________

What's the word?

1. 

The Caribbean is also famous for its __________.

2. Ein entfernter Vulkan ist für Touristen nicht gefährlich.

A __________ volcano is not dangerous for tourists.

3. 

Sometimes you can see __________ behind them.

4. Man kann auch den Donner hören.

You can hear __________ too.

5. Wenn kein Sturm in der Nähe ist, können sich die Menschen am Strand entspannen.

When there is no storm __________, people can __________ on the beach.

6. Einige Touristen feiern den ganzen Tag und essen Meeresfrüchte am Strand.

Some tourists __________ all day and eat __________ on the beach.

10 Put a circle around the odd one out and write it in German.

1. ship • volcano • ferry • boat __________
2. thunder • lightning • seafood • storm __________
3. work • study • relax • clean __________

11 Look at the picture and complete the sentences.

Sue and Peter want to find __________ (1) today. It's hot on the __________ (2) beach. But there is a storm nearby. Peter does not like the sound of __________ (3). Sue is worried about the __________ (4). Maybe they should go home.

What's the word?

1. Meine Eltern sind ziemlich konservativ. — My parents are quite ______________.
2. Ihnen ist Religion sehr wichtig. — ______________ is very important to them.
3. Sie haben einen starken Glauben. — Their ______________ is strong.
4. Sie haben hart dafür gearbeitet, um in die Gesellschaft hineinzupassen. — They worked hard to ______________.
5. Als mein Bruder 16 war, hat er sich als schwul geoutet. — When my brother was 16, he ______________ ______________.
6.  — It was a ______________ to the whole family when he told them.
7. Sie wollten nie auffallen. — They never wanted to ______________.
8. Aber ihre Werte helfen ihnen, locker zu sein. — But their ______________ help them to be easy-going.
9. Jetzt sprechen sie überall darüber. — Now they talk about it ______________.
10. Sie sind nicht so altmodisch, wie ich dachte. — They are not as ______________ as I thought.

12 Find nine words. (↓ and →) Write them in English and German.

S	V	A	L	U	E	S	W	E	O	R
F	T	Z	W	S	O	P	A	S	L	D
A	F	G	X	T	S	T	A	N	D	H
I	J	K	A	A	X	C	V	B	-	N
T	P	O	L	N	R	E	W	Q	F	A
H	F	D	T	D	H	J	K	G	A	Y
E	I	S	H	O	C	K	T	U	S	E
C	T	X	C	U	B	N	M	Q	H	W
K	I	R	T	T	U	I	O	P	I	A
S	N	F	R	E	L	I	G	I	O	N
R	N	S	P	E	C	T	G	H	N	K
E	V	E	R	Y	W	H	E	R	E	N
S	V	I	M	L	O	R	C	H	D	S

____
____
____
____
____
____
____
____
____

What's the word?

1. Gestern Abend surfte Lisa im Internet. — ______ Lisa surfed the internet.
2. Sie glaubt an Freundschaft im Internet. — She believes in internet ______.
3. Ich denke, Onlinefreundschaften sind kompliziert. — I think online friendships are ______.
4. Man weiß nicht, ob man auf die Dinge, die die Leute online schreiben, vertrauen kann. — You don't know if you can ______ the things people write online.
5. Es ist eine Anstrengung, online den richtigen Mann oder die richtige Frau zu finden. — It's a ______ to find the right man or woman online.
6. Aber die Zahl der Leute, die ihren Partner im Internet finden, steigt an. — But the number of people who find their partner on the internet ______.
7.  — Many people ______ a person they've met online.

13 Put in the right words.

complicated | conservative | friendship | gay | last night | relax | rely on | shock | values

E-MAIL

Dear Sue,

Thanks for your message. I saw it ______. I hope this isn't a ______ for you, but I'm ______. I'm only looking for ______. You say you aren't ______, and I think you have good ______. So being friends won't be too ______, will it? You can trust me and ______ me as a friend. Now that I told you, I hope we can ______.

Please write to me soon.

Love, Phil

14 Match the opposites. ⟷

1. relax
2. modern
3. fit in
4. easy
5. boring

a) old-fashioned
b) extraordinary
c) complicated
d) be nervous
e) stand out

What's the word?

1. 

Susan wants to study ________________ when she finishes school.

2. Sie möchte unabhängig sein und ihr eigenes Geld verdienen.

She wants to be ____________________ and earn her own money.

3. Sie schrieb in den sozialen Medien über ihre Pläne. Viele Leute kommentierten dies.

She wrote about her plans on social media. Many people ______________________ it.

4. Es gab eine interessante Aussage.

There was an interesting __________________.

5. Jemand sagte, es gebe nicht genügend Krankenschwestern und dies sei ein ständiges Problem.

Someone said there weren't enough nurses and that it was a ________________ problem.

6. Ich denke, er hat recht. Einerseits gibt es so viele alte Menschen, die Krankenpflege brauchen.

I think he's right. ________________________, there are so many old people who need nursing.

7. Andererseits verdienen Krankenpfleger nicht viel Geld. Deshalb wollen nur wenige Leute den Job machen.

_________________________, nurses don't earn a lot of money, so very few people want to do the job.

15 Put in the right words.

complicated | independent | nursing | on the one hand | on the other hand

Hi. You said that something was ______________?
Yes. My grandpa isn't well.

What's wrong with him?

He isn't ____________________ any more.

Oh, no! What happened?

He needs to go into a _______________ home.

Doesn't he want to go?

Well, _______________________, he can't pay for it. _______________________, he needs constant nursing.

What's the word?

1. Es gibt viel Gewalt in Sams Straße. — There is a lot of ________________ in Sam's street.
2. Sein Vater starb in einer Schießerei. — His dad died in a ________________.
3.  — His brother takes ________________.
4. Er hat Angst, dass bald wieder Gewalt ausbrechen könnte. — He is afraid violence could ________________ again soon.
5. Obwohl Sam an Freundschaft glaubt, ist sein Leben schwer. — ________________ Sam believes in friendship, his life is hard.
6. Sam geht gern zur Schule. Er weiß, dass es ein Privileg ist. Andere Jungen in seiner Straße müssen stattdessen arbeiten gehen. — Sam likes going to school. He knows it's a ________________. Other boys in his street have to work instead.

16 Match the sentences with the picture.

The family is happy although they are poor. | The tourists have many privileges. | They are selling drugs. | They don't like violence. | He listens to music everywhere. | He was hurt in a shooting.

1. ________________________________
2. ________________________________
3. ________________________________
4. ________________________________
5. ________________________________
6. ________________________________

What's the word?

1. Barbados ist in der Karibik. — ____________ is in the Caribbean.
2. Das Leben auf Barbados war früher brutal. — Life on Barbados was ____________ in the past.
3.  — There were pirates who kept their ____________ on their ships.
4. Sie ließen die Gefangenen auf dem Fußboden der Kabine allein. — They left the prisoners ____________ on the ____________ of the ____________.
5. Das war eine schreckliche Strafe. — This was a terrible ____________.
6. Die Gefangenen riefen um Hilfe. — The prisoners ____________ for help.
7. Aber es gab keine Reaktion. Die Tür öffnete sich nicht. — But there was no ____________. The door did not ____________.

17 Put a circle around the odd one out and write it in German.

1. workers • students • prisoners • teachers ____________
2. cry • run • walk • jump ____________
3. polite • nice • friendly • brutal ____________
4. table • bed • floor • chair ____________

18 Put in the right words.

although | Barbados | brutal | cabin | cried | prisoners | punishment | reaction

1. There was a ship in the Caribbean near ____________.
2. Some ____________ pirates saw the ship. They wanted to take ____________.
3. The passengers were afraid of the pirates' ____________.
4. Some of the women tried to hide in the ____________.
5. ____________ they ____________ for help, there was no ____________.

What's the word?

1.  My neighbour had an old ______________ in the attic.
2. Sie zeigte in den Himmel. — It was ______________ at the ______________.
3. Eines Tages drehte er sie herum. — One day he ______________ it ______________.
4. Ich erkannte die Gefahr: Die Kanone zeigte jetzt auf unser Haus. — I ______________ the danger. The cannon was now pointing at our house.
5. Ich hatte große Angst. — I was ______________.
6. Ich musste mir etwas einfallen lassen. — I had to ______________ something.
7. Mein Nachbar fuhr damit fort, seine Kanone immer wieder herumzudrehen. — My neighbour ______________ to turn his cannon around again and again.
8. Eines Tages kam eine Krankenschwester und nahm ihn mit. Manchmal denke ich, er hatte Glück, dass jemand kam und sich um ihn kümmerte. — One day a nurse came and took him with her. Sometimes I think he ______________ someone came and took care of him.

19 Put in the right words.

around | away | in | of | of | out

1. turn ______________
2. think ______________
3. take one's breath ______________
4. break ______________
5. terrified ______________
6. fit ______________

20 Put in the right words.

cannons | crying | lucky | pirates | prisoner | punishment | recognise | sky | terrified | think of

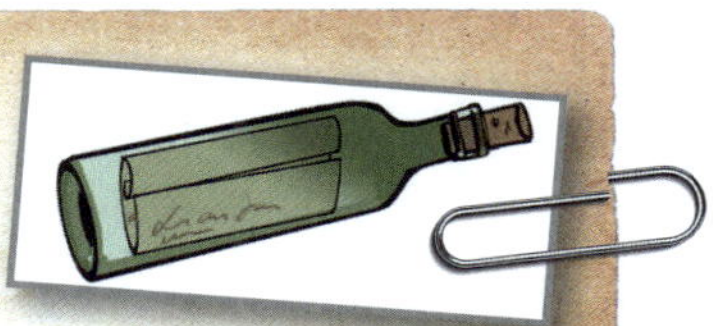

Dear friend,

Please help me! I'm a ______________ in the Caribbean. Some ______________ have taken me away from my ship. I am ______________ because they always point at the ______________. I think this will be their ______________. I can't ______________ a way to escape. I'm ______________ for help, but only the ______________ can hear me. If I am ______________, another ship will ______________ the pirate ship and help me.

Captain Henry

What's the word?

1. Von meinen Eltern habe ich gelernt, kein Geld zu verschwenden. — I learned from my parents not to ______________ money.
2. Sie sagten, Reichtum kommt durch harte Arbeit. — They said ______________ comes with hard work.
3. Sie erwarteten Engagement von mir und anderen. — They expected ______________ from me and others.
4. Aber sie übernahmen auch Verantwortung für arme Leute. — But they also took ______________ for poor people.
5. Sie zeigten Solidarität und halfen ihnen, einen Job zu finden. — They showed ______________ and helped them to find a job.

21 Complete the words.

-ility | -ing | -ment | -ment | -ship | -tion | -ty | -ty

1. solidari______________
2. responsib______________
3. punish______________
4. reac______________
5. commit______________
6. hones______________
7. nurs______________
8. friend______________

22 Complete the crossword.

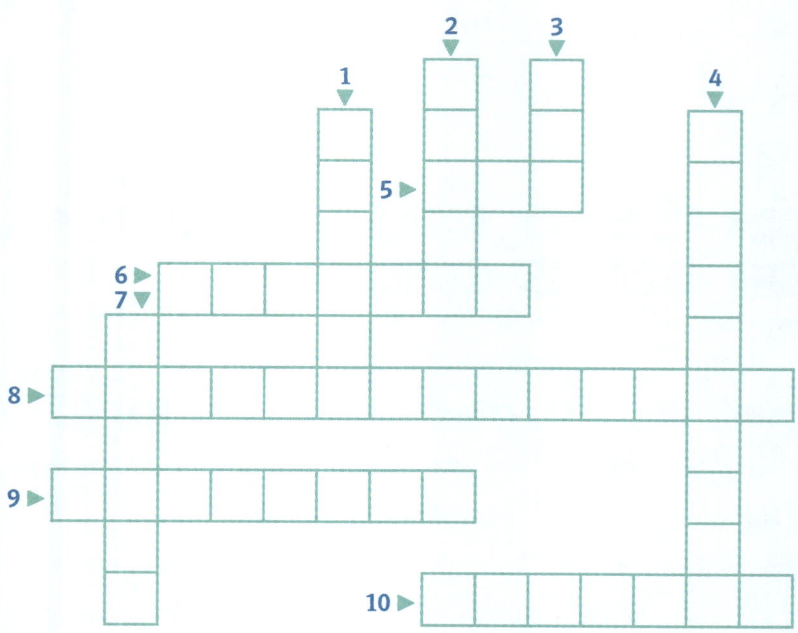

Down ▼:

1. something that was used on ships for fighting
2. Don't … food!
3. When men love other men, they are …
4. If you really want this job, you have to show …
7. a lot of money

Across ►:

5. The stars are in the …
6. … and lightning
8. adjective = responsible
   noun = …
9. English for *obwohl*
10. adjective = honest
    noun = …

What's the word?

1. Die Tür flog auf. — The door ____________.
2. Es war einer der Piraten. Er hatte einen bösen Ausdruck im Gesicht. — It was one of the pirates. He had an ____________ ____________ on his face.
3. Die junge Gefangene wollte ihn nicht ansehen. Sie schaute stattdessen durch das Bullauge. Sie wartete auf Hilfe. — The young prisoner did not want to look at him. She looked through the ____________ instead. She was waiting for help.
4. Sie hatte Angst und dachte, der Pirat würde sie erschießen. — She was afraid and thought the pirate would ____________ her.
5. Der Pirat war amüsiert. — The pirate was ____________.
6. Es war das Jahr 1625. Damals gab es in der Karibik viele Piraten. Sie nahmen gern britische Gefangene. — It was 1625. There were a lot of pirates in the Caribbean ____________. They liked to take British prisoners.

23 Look at the pictures and write the words.

1. evil ____________
2. ____________
3. ____________

24 Make sentences. Put the words in the right order.

1. door • Suddenly • open • and • mother • the • flew • room. • my • entered • the

____

2. wasn't • look. • and • I • gave • amused • evil • her • an

____

3. didn't • know • I • time. • would • become • a • I • musician • famous • at • that

____

4. can • sharks • see • the • through • You • porthole. • the

____

What's the word?

1. Der Pirat nahm die Gefangene mit aufs Schiffsdeck. — The pirate took the prisoner up to the ____________.
2. Sie fiel auf den Boden. Sie brauchte einen Moment, bis sie wieder aufstehen konnte. — She fell on the floor. ______________________ to get up again.
3. Sie konnte einen Schuss hören. — She could hear a ____________.
4. Ein anderer Pirat feuerte weitere Schüsse in die Luft ab. — Another pirate ____________ more shots into the air.
5. Da wusste sie, sie würde über eine Schiffsplanke ins Wasser getrieben werden. — That was when she knew she would have to ______________________.

25 Look at the pictures and write the words.

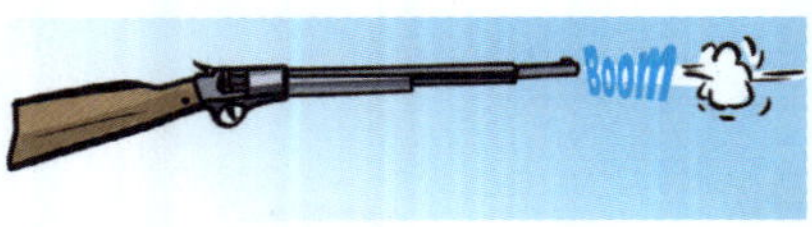

1. fire a ____________________ 2. ____________________ 3. ____________________

26 Put a circle around the right words.

1. He took no responsibility (for • to • with) the fire in the office.
2. Sam shows great commitment (of • to • with) his work.
3. Jerry is gay. At first he was afraid he wouldn't fit (in • out • with).
4. I feel no solidarity (in • of • with) rude people.
5. She has faith (in • out • with) her friends.
6. She can always rely (of • on • for) them.
7. When you are in trouble, you have to think (from • with • of) something.
8. I was terrified (from • with • of) him (at • in • of) that time.

What's the word?

1. In Südafrika sprechen viele Menschen Englisch. — Many people speak English in ____________________.
2. Nelson Mandela war der erste schwarze Präsident. — Nelson Mandela was the first black ____________________.
3. Der Sitz der Regierung ist in Pretoria. — The ______________ of government is in Pretoria.
4.  — The money from tourists and ________________ mines is very important for South Africa.
5. In Südafrika kann man auf Safari gehen. — You can go on a ______________ in South Africa.
6. Auf einer Safari kann man wilde Tiere sehen. — On a safari you can see ____________ animals.
7. Viele Touristen gehen auf Safari, um Löwen zu sehen. — Many tourists go on a safari to see ____________.
8. Die meisten von ihnen wollen auch Nashörner sehen. — Most of them want to see ______________ too.

1 Look at the pictures and write the words.

1. ____________________

2. ____________________

3. ____________________

2 Make sentences. Put the words in the right order.

1. year. • next • to • South Africa • go • want • I • to

____

2. film • about • yesterday. • diamond • mine • a • a • saw • I

____

3. Rhinos • animals. • lions • are • wild • and

____

4. has • country • capitals. • The • three

____

What's the word?

1. Der bekannteste Nationalpark ist der Kruger-Nationalpark. — The most famous ____________________ is Kruger National Park.

2. Er ist ein Naturreservat, in dem die Menschen Tiere, Pflanzen und Landschaft schützen. — It is a ____________________ where people protect plants, animals and the landscape.

3. Südafrikaner lieben ihr Land und dessen Tiere. — ____________________ love their country and its animals.

4. 

The *Daily Sun* is one of the biggest ____________________ in South Africa.

5. In den Medien kann man jeden Tag Berichte über die Tierwelt Südafrikas lesen. — You can read ______________ about South Africa's wildlife in the ____________ every day.

3 Put in the right words.

national parks | newspaper | report | rhinos | safari

The Cape Town Observer

Cape Town's oldest ________________

On a ____________

See the last ____________ in our ____________________

A ____________ by Jan de Mool

4 Match the sentence parts.

1. South Africa's population is
2. South Africans are proud
3. South Africa is famous
4. There are many nature reserves
5. Newspapers report about

a) of their first black president, Nelson Mandela.
b) for its national parks.
c) the government, sports and wildlife.
d) mostly African.
e) to protect animals.

What's the word?

1. Die Niederländer kamen vor etwa 400 Jahren nach Südafrika. — ______________ came to South Africa about 400 years ago.
2. Apartheid ist ein trauriger Teil der Geschichte Südafrikas. — ______________ is a sad part of South African history.
3.  — Apartheid ______________ black and white people.
4. Nelson Mandela wollte ein neues Südafrika gründen. — Nelson Mandela wanted to ______________ a new South Africa.
5. Er wollte einen Staat gründen, in dem Schwarze und Weiße in Frieden zusammenleben können. — He wanted to build a ______________ in which black and white people could live together in peace.

5 Match the words and their meanings.

1. apartheid
2. media
3. build
4. nation
5. separate

a) country
b) make or start something
c) a system that separated black and white people
d) newspapers, magazines, TV and the internet
e) put into two groups

6 Put in the right words.

apartheid | media | nations | separated | the Dutch

1. ______________ ended in 1994.
2. In many countries the ______________ reported about the end of apartheid.
3. Now black and white people are not ______________ by law any more.
4. I hope that one day all ______________ will live together in peace.
5. ______________ built a colony in South Africa 400 years ago.

What's the word?

1. Townships sind sehr arme Wohngegenden. — ________________ are very poor areas.
2. Reiche Leute leben oft in bewachten Wohnanlagen mit hoher Sicherheit. — Rich people often live in ________________ with high ________________.
3. Während der Apartheid gab es Krieg. — There was a ____________ during apartheid.
4. Südafrika ist jetzt ein demokratisches Land. — Now South Africa is a ________________ country.
5.  — People can ____________ for the president.
6. Die Verfassung gibt dem Staat, der Regierung und den Menschen Regeln. — The ________________ gives rules to the country, the government and the people.
7. Alle fünf Jahre gibt es Präsidentschaftswahlen. — There are ________________ for president every five years.

7 Choose the right word.

constitution | democratic | townships | separate | vote | war

1. nation • rules • ________________
2. city • gated communities • ____________
3. president • elections • ____________
4. good • free • ________________
5. fight • soldier • ________________
6. apartheid • black people • ____________

8 Complete the two mind maps.

constitution | democratic | election | internet | newspaper | report | TV | vote

What's the word?

1. In Südafrika müssen Familien für Privatschulen zahlen. — In South Africa families have to pay for ______ schools.
2. Viele arme Kinder brechen die Schule ab und versuchen, Arbeit zu finden. — Many poor children ______ school and try to find work.
3. Ihre Eltern denken nicht an die Folgen. — Their parents don't think of the ______.
4. Einige Kinder sind Opfer einer schlechten Familiensituation. — Some children are the ______ of a bad family situation.
5. Arme Familien haben oft keine Krankenversicherung. — Poor families often don't have ______ ______.
6. Reiche Kinder können auf Privatschulen gehen. Sie sind gut ausgebildet. — Rich children can go to private schools. They are ______.
7. Arme Kinder gehen stattdessen auf öffentliche Schulen. — Poor children go to ______ instead.

9 What are they saying? Complete the sentences.

consequences | dropped out of | health insurance | private school | state school | well-educated

1 My parents are poor so I had to go to a ______. But I ______ ______ school. I didn't think of the ______ at the time.

2 My parents are ______ and earn a lot of money. I can go to a ______ ______. My parents also have good ______.

10 Put a circle around the right words.

1. Poor children often (drop out of • separate from) school to earn money for the family.
2. They usually don't get skilled jobs. They are the (elections • victims) of the system.
3. Rich families often live in gated communities because they want (consequences • security).
4. Their children usually are (democratic • well-educated), get better jobs and earn more money.

What's the word?

1. Leute, die zur Mittelschicht gehören, schicken ihre Kinder auf öffentliche Schulen. — People who ____________ send their children to state schools.
2. Viele Leute denken, dass es nicht gerecht ist, dass man für eine gute Bildung zahlen muss. — Many people think it isn't ____________ that you have to pay for a good education.
3. Kinder, die auf Privatschulen gehen, sind privilegiert. — Children who can go to private schools are ____________.
4. Ich denke, alle Kinder sollten im Leben die gleichen Chancen haben. — I think all children should have ____________ opportunities in life.
5. Kinder in armen Gegenden fühlen sich oft nicht sicher. — Children in poor areas often don't feel ____________.
6. Ihre Situation macht sie zu Außenseitern der Gesellschaft. — Their situation often makes them ____________ in society.

11 Match the opposites. ↔

1. outcast
2. be privileged
3. fair
4. equal
5. feel secure

a) not OK
b) not the same
c) have few opportunities
d) be afraid
e) part of a group

12 Make sentences. Put the words in the right order.

1. who • People • car • often • have • a • middle-class • and • house. • are • a

____

2. children • Germany • are • Many • privileged. • in

____

3. school. • feels • an • Lefa • outcast • at • like

____

4. equal • are • All • law. • people • under • the

____

What's the word?

1. Mein Vater arbeitet auf dem Bau. Letzte Woche hat er einen Unfall beobachtet.

   My father works in ______________________. He saw an accident last week.

2. 

   So he wrote a letter to the ______________________.

3. Er begann mit „Sehr geehrte Damen und Herren, …“.

   He started the letter with ‘______________________ ______________’.

4. Er schrieb, was er beobachtet hatte, und beendete den Brief mit „Mit freundlichen Grüßen“ und seinem Namen.

   He wrote about what he had seen and ended the letter with ‘______________________’ and his name.

5. Papa erzählte mir, dass er immer noch Rückblenden von einem Unfall hat, den er als Jugendlicher hatte. Ich glaube, deshalb wollte er nicht aufs Polizeirevier gehen.

   Dad told me that he still has ____________________ of an accident he had as a teenager. I think that is why he didn't want to go to the police station.

13 Match the sentences with the pictures.

- Tsire cannot play football for two months.
- My cousin Tsire was the victim of an accident.
- The driver of the other car was a priviliged white man.
- The driver was taken to the police station.
- It is still not clear what caused the accident.
- He has flashbacks about the accident.

1. ______________________________ ______________________________

2. ______________________________ ______________________________ ______________________________

3. ______________________________ ______________________________

4. ______________________________ ______________________________

5. ______________________________ ______________________________

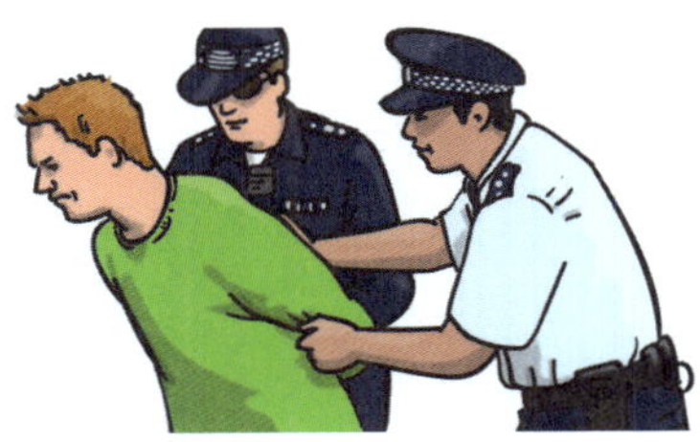

6. ______________________________ ______________________________

What's the word?

1. Mein Bruder hatte letzte Woche einen Autounfall. Dieser hat ihn zu Tode erschreckt.

   My brother had a car accident last week.

   It ______________________________.

2. Jetzt hat er manchmal Albträume.

   Now he has ________________ sometimes.

3. Er kann nicht glauben, dass irgendein Idiot ein Leben in einer Sekunde zerstören kann.

   He can't believe ___________________ could ruin a life in one second.

4. Er fühlt sich schuldig, weil der Fahrer des Autos hinter ihm auch verletzt wurde.

   He feels ___________ because the driver of the car behind him got hurt too.

5. Wir sind arm und daher bekommt er keine Behandlung gegen seine Albträume.

   We are poor so he doesn't get any ___________ for his nightmares.

6. Wir haben weder eine Krankenversicherung noch genug Geld, um selbst für die Behandlung zu zahlen.

   We have ____________ health insurance __________ enough money to pay for the treatment ourselves.

14 Put in the right words.

drop out of | frightened the hell out of | guilty | health insurance | neither ... nor | nightmares | Police Station | Sir or Madam | treatment | Yours faithfully

Dear ____________________,

I am writing to you because my husband had a car accident near Durban ____________________.

He was not ____________. I saw the accident. The noise ______________________________

me. I have _________________ now. My husband cannot pay for the ________________ he

needs because he can ______________ work __________ get _____________________.

We have five children and we cannot pay for the flat and food for all of us, so the oldest will have

to _________________ school. Can you please help us?

_____________________,

Sikabe Mbongo

What's the word?

1. In manchen Nationalparks gibt es Sandebenen.	In some national parks there are sand ________________ .
2. Um die Nationalparks wurden Zäune errichtet.	________________ were built around the national parks.
3. Einige Parks sind auch Wüsten.	Some parks are ________________ too.
4. Sümpfe können gefährlich sein, weil das Land dort nass ist.	________________ can be dangerous because the land is wet there.
5. Auch Gebirge können Teil eines Naturreservats sein.	________________ can be part of a nature reserve too.
6. Ranger begannen ihre Arbeit, als der Kruger-Nationalpark 1927 eröffnete.	________________ started working when Kruger National Park ________________ in 1927.
7. Seitdem beschützen sie die Tiere im Park.	They have protected the animals in the park ________________ .
8. Ihr Ziel ist es, Tiere wie Elefanten und Nashörner zu erhalten.	Their goal is to ________________ animals like elephants and rhinos.
9. Der Kruger-Nationalpark wurde nach Präsident Kruger benannt, der von 1883 bis 1900 Präsident von Südafrika war.	Kruger Park was ________________ after President Kruger, who was president of South Africa from 1883 to 1900.

15 Look at the pictures and write the words.

1. ____________________

2. ____________________

3. ____________________

4. ____________________

5. ____________________

6. ____________________

What's the word?

1. Natur und Tiere sind sehr wichtig für den Tourismus in Südafrika. — Nature and animals are very important for South African ________.
2. Besucher müssen einen Führer anheuern. Sie dürfen nicht allein gehen. — Visitors must ________ a guide. They mustn't go on their own.
3. Sie dürfen auch ihren Abfall nicht im Park zurücklassen. — They also mustn't ________ their waste in the park.
4. Die meisten Touristen möchten die Tiere beobachten. Aber manche wollen sie jagen. — Most tourists want to watch the animals. But some want to ________ them.
5. Manche Jäger jagen Elefanten wegen ihres Elfenbeins, was nicht erlaubt ist. — Some hunt elephants for their ________, which is not allowed.
6. Die Regierung regelt die Zahl der Jäger und Touristen. — The government ________ the number of ________ and tourists.
7.  — That is why the numbers of ________ are going up again.
8. Büffel können auch gejagt werden. — ________ can be hunted too.
9. Elefanten, Leoparden, Nashörner und Büffel sind Wild. — Elephants, leopards, rhinos and buffaloes are ________.

16 Look at the pictures and write the words.

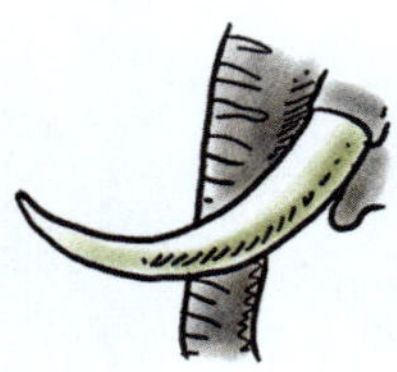

1. ________ 2. ________ 3. ________

17 Put a circle around the right words.

1. Elephants, buffaloes and rhinos are (game • play).
2. There are (leopards • kangaroos) in South Africa too.
3. National parks are very important for (tourism • factories).
4. Hunters are not allowed to (hire • hunt) for ivory.
5. Rules (conserve • regulate) what tourists can and can't do in the parks.

What's the word?

1. Die Ranger behandeln die Tiere mit Respekt.	Rangers ____________ the animals with ____________.
2. Jedes Lebewesen verdient Respekt.	Every creature ____________ respect.
3. Wenn man sieht, dass ein Tier nicht gut behandelt wird, sollte man eingreifen.	If you see that an animal is not treated well, you should ____________.
4. Jagen, das gegen das Gesetz verstößt, nennt man Wilderei.	Hunting that is against the law is called ____________.
5. In der letzten Ausgabe der Zeitschrift „Wild Africa" war ein Bericht über Wilderei.	There was a report about poaching in the latest ____________ of the *Wild Africa* magazine.
6. Ich habe gelesen, dass die neue Regierung jetzt handelt und die Zeit für Wilderei abgelaufen ist.	I read that the new government is taking action and that time for poaching is ____________.

18 Put a circle around the odd one out and write it in German.

1. good • respect • fair • equal ____________
2. sit • take action • wait • sleep ____________
3. buffalo • rhino • treat • leopard ____________
4. ranger • nurse • hunter • tourism ____________

19 Match the sentence parts.

1. Have you read the latest	a) against the law.
2. There was a report	b) to be treated with respect.
3. Poaching is	c) edition of the *Wild Africa* magazine?
4. The government has taken	d) for hunters is up.
5. I think the time	e) action to protect wild animals.
6. Animals deserve	f) on poaching.

What's the word?

1. Ich hatte die Grundschule im Sommer beendet und würde bald auf die Johannesburger Stadtschule gehen.
   I had finished ______________ in the summer and would soon start at Johannesburg City School.
2. Im September waren die Ferien vorbei und das neue Schuljahr begann.
   In September the holidays were ______________ and the new school year ______________.
3. In der Schule gab es einen richtigen Spielplatz, nicht nur trockenen Erdboden zum Spielen.
   There was a real playground at the school, not just some dry ______________ to play on.
4. Sie hatten auch einen großen Sportplatz.
   They also had a large ______________.
5. Er war besser als der an meiner alten Schule, wo ich oft hingefallen bin und mir am Hintern wehgetan habe.
   It was better than the one at my old school, where I had often fallen and hurt my ______________.
6. Mein Klassenlehrer war ein Schwarzer.
   My class teacher was a ______________.
7. An seinem ersten Tag an der Schule waren draußen vor dem Schulgebäude Demonstranten.
   On his first day at the school there were ______________ outside the school building.
8. Ich mag es nicht, wenn Leute gegen Schwarze protestieren, nur weil sie Schwarze sind.
   I don't like it when people ______________ against black people just because they are black.
9. Ich hoffe, unser Lehrer muss sich nicht allein um diese Leute kümmern.
   I hope our teacher doesn't have to ______________ those people alone.

20 Look at the pictures and complete the sentences.

1. The year is ______________.

2. There are many ______________ in the streets today.

3. My little sister goes to ______________.

4. Zoe is my best friend. She's ______________.

5. My Saturday job ______________ in October.

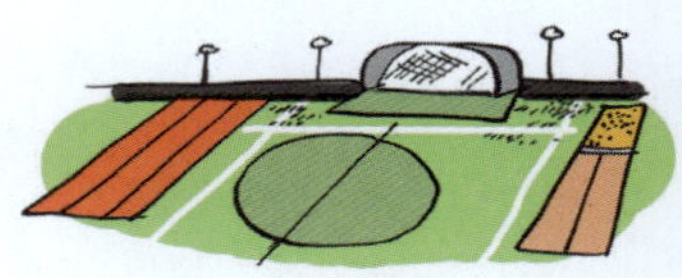

6. The ______________ of our school is quite large.

What's the word?

1. Mein Klassenlehrer ist auch der Schulleiter meiner neuen Schule. — My class teacher also is the ____________ of my new school.
2. Er warnte uns, unsere Smartphones während des Unterrichts nicht zu benutzen. — He ____________ us not to use our smartphones during class.
3.  — We were just talking about my favourite animals, ____________.
4. Ein Junge versuchte, sein Telefon unter dem Tisch zu benutzen. — One boy ____________ to use his phone under the desk.
5. Der Lehrer sah ihn an und fragte: „Benutzt irgendjemand gerade sein Telefon?" — The teacher looked in his direction and asked, "Is ____________ using his or her phone at the moment?"
6. Er meinte es ernst. Er scherzte nicht. — He was serious. He wasn't ____________.
7. Aber während der Pausen lässt er uns in Ruhe. — But he ____________ during the breaks.
8. Nach der letzten Klassenarbeit schaute er traurig, schüttelte den Kopf und sagte: „Ihr habt alle ziemlich schlecht abgeschnitten." — After the last class test he looked sad, ____________ ____________ and said, "All of you did pretty badly."
9.  — But then he ____________. He was only joking.

21 Put in the right words.

Jenny's blog – the pink cat

Hi there. How is it going?

Holiday time is ____________ and I'm back at school. My older brother's friend Kagiso visited us during the holidays. They went to ____________ together. My father was the ____________ there. Kagiso was the first ____________ boy at Jan's school. Some parents ____________ outside the school building and their kids ____________ to push Kagiso. But Dad ____________ them to ____________. Kagiso is really good at rugby and he's cool. He ____________ with me all the time. When he left, he ____________ at me …

black
joked
headteacher
up
primary school
smiled
leave him alone
protested
tried
warned

What's the word?

1. Eltern sind unverantwortlich, wenn sie sich nicht um ihre Kinder kümmern.
   Parents are ____________ if they don't care for their children.

2. Einige arme Familien sind abhängig von dem Geld, das ihre Kinder verdienen.
   Some poor families are ____________ on the money their children earn.

3. Arme Kinder haben oft weniger Chancen als reiche Kinder. Sie sind benachteiligt.
   Poor children often don't have as many chances as rich kids. They are ____________.

4. 
   Some of them work for rich people. They look after their gardens and ____________.

5. Mein Nachbar hat eine eigene Quelle in seinem Garten.
   My neighbour has his own ____________ in his garden.

6. Die reichen Leute leben in den Hügeln, aber die meisten armen Familien wohnen in Townships unten im Tal.
   The rich people live in the hills, but most poor families live in townships down in the ____________.

7. Der Hauptteil unserer Stadt liegt im Tal.
   The ____________ part of our town is in the valley.

8. 
   Huge ____________ grow along the main road.

22 Look at the pictures and complete the sentences.

1. A driver is ____________ when he drinks and drives.
2. His parents are poor and he is ____________.
3. The baby is ____________ on its mother.

23 Match the opposites. ↔

1. responsible
2. dependent
3. hill
4. privileged
5. protest
6. begin

a) end
b) underprivileged
c) agree
d) irresponsible
e) independent
f) valley

What's the word?

1. Letztes Jahr wechselten Mama und Papa sich ab, mich von der Schule abzuholen. — Last year Mum and Dad ____________ picking me up from school.
2.  — Mum ____________ for rich families and Dad looked after their gardens.
3. Die beiden arbeiteten sehr hart. — ____________ worked very hard.
4. Eine Familie, die van Betuws, haben einen Rasensprenger, um ihren Garten schön und grün zu halten. — One family, the van Betuws, have a ____________ to keep their garden nice and green.
5. Ich war mit Papa gern dort und schnitt lustige Grimassen unter dem Rasensprenger. — I liked to be there with Dad and ____________ ____________ under the sprinkler.
6. Die van Betuws hatten auch einen kleinen Hund. Manchmal versuchte er, Leute anzugreifen, und rannte wie ein Wilder umher. — The van Betuws also had a little dog. Sometimes it tried to attack people and ran around like a ____________.
7. Aber Papa hat einen Fehler gemacht und jetzt ist er lebenslang im Gefängnis. — But Dad did something wrong and now he is in prison ____________.
8. 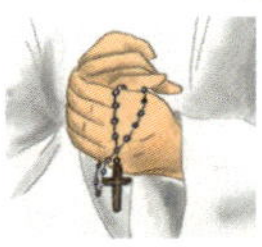 — This is why I ____________ for him and our family every night.

24 Put a circle around the right words.

1. My best friend Malik and his father go to church every Sunday to (talk • pray).
2. Jane made funny (faces • feet) at me.
3. I have two older brothers. The (two • main) of them are good at rugby.
4. They are taking (time • turns) helping Dad in the garden.
5. Nelson Mandela was put in prison (for life • always) because he wanted to end apartheid.

25 Complete the words.

A A E E E E E E E I I I I I I
O O O U U

1. _r_n
2. t_k_ t_rns
3. f_r l_f_
4. pr_y
5. _rr_sp_ns_bl_
6. _nd_rpr_v_l_g_d

What's the word?

1. 

We went to Addo Elephant National Park at the beginning of the ________________.

2. Als wir zu den Tieren gingen, hielt Mama meine Hand richtig fest.

When we walked to the animals, Mum held my hand really ______________.

3. Aber sie konnte mich nicht davon abhalten, vor den großen Tieren Angst zu haben.

But she couldn't ________________________ being afraid of the big animals.

4. Ein Ranger wandte sich mir zu und fragte: „Möchtest du den kleinen Elefanten füttern?"

A ranger _______________________ and asked, "Do you want to feed the little elephant?"

5. Ich schüttelte den Kopf und wurde rot.

I shook my head and __________________.

6. Er war wirklich nett und sagte: „Hab' keine Angst. Mach es schrittweise."

He was really nice and said, "Don't be afraid. Take it ____________________________."

7. Also holte ich tief Luft und streckte langsam meine Hand aus.

So I ______________________________ and slowly held out my hand.

26 Look at the pictures and complete the sentences.

1. I was nervous, but my friend held my hand very __________.

2. When the teacher asked Linda if she knew the answer, she ________________.

3. When I called Sam, he ______________________.

27 Complete the sentences.

at | for | from | of | on | to | with

1. The boys _________ the bus turned _________ me and smiled.
2. The two _________ them looked really cool.
3. It's always good to take one step _________ a time.
4. Teachers have to deal ___________ naughty kids.
5. My friends stopped me ____________ making a big mistake.
6. My neighbour is in prison __________ life because he started a shooting and killed someone.

What's the word?

1. China ist ein faszinierendes Land. — China ______ is a fascinating country.
2. Dort eröffnen jede Woche riesige neue Einkaufszentren. — Huge new Mall ______ open there every week.
3. Aber es gibt auch Straßenmärkte mit Essensständen und Wahrsagern. — But there are also street markets with food stalls and fortune tellers ______.
4. Viele Kunden fahren mit dem Auto in die Einkaufszentren. Das verursacht Luftverschmutzung. — Many customers drive to the malls. This causes air pollution ______.
5. Wenn viel Verschmutzung in der Luft ist, sieht der Himmel grau aus. Man nennt das Smog. — If there is a lot of air pollution, the sky looks grey. People call it smog ______.
6. Smog verursacht Gesundheitsprobleme für die Menschen in großen Städten wie Hongkong. — Smog causes health ______ problems for people in big cities like Hong Kong.
7. Obwohl Hongkong Verschmutzungsprobleme hat, ist es eine unglaubliche Stadt. Sie ist eine Mischung aus Osten und Westen. — Although Hong Kong has pollution problems, it's an amazing city. It's a mixture ______ of East and West.

1 Look at the pictures and write the words.

1. fortune tellers ______

2. Mall ______

3. China ______

2 Find the words. Write them in English and German.

pollution|smog|health|China|mall|mixture

pollution → Verschmutzung ______
smog → smog ______
health → Gesundheit ______
China → China ______
mall → Einkaufszentrum ______
mixture → Mischung ______

What's the word?

1. Leute, die beim Einkaufen immer neue Plastiktüten verwenden, verursachen immer mehr Verschmutzung.
   People who use new plastic bags every time they go shopping crecles ______ more pollution.

2. Wir sollten die Zahl der Plastiktüten, die wir verwenden, reduzieren.
   We should try to reduce ______ the number of plastic bags we use.

3. Some types of plastic can be recycle ______.

4. Smog ist der Grund, warum die Regierung versucht, die Zahl der Autos in den belebten Teilen der Stadt zu reduzieren.
   Smog is why the government tries to reduce the number of cars in the ______ parts of the city.

5. Jeden Tag gibt es viele Medienberichte über Smog.
   There are a lot of media ______ reports about smog every day.

3 Put in the right words.

busiest | China | fortune tellers | health | malls | media | mixture | reduce | recycle | pollution | smog

E-MAIL

Dear Mum and Dad,

Hong Kong is really fascinating! It's a ______ of East and West. It's the ______ city in China. It became part of ______ in 1997, but it has a special status. There are so many shops, markets and ______. They sell clothes, smartphones and Chinese food. You can go shopping day and night. But Hong Kong is also famous for its busy ______ industry.

But because of all the people, the city has a problem with ______ and smog. The people here try to ______ waste and to ______ as much as they can. But the ______ is really bad. Sometimes the sky is so grey you can't see the sun. Smog can cause ______ problems.

Let's hope that the ______ who say the air will be better in 2025 are right. ☺

Love,

Danny

What's the word?

1. Wie viele Punkte würdest du China für seine Aktivitäten zur Reduzierung von Verschmutzung geben?	How many ______________ would you give China for its activities to reduce pollution?
2. 0 1 2 3 4 5 6 7 8 9 10	On a ______________ of one to ten I would give it a three.
3. Die Europäer versuchen, die Verschmutzung auf andere Art und Weise zu verringern.	Europeans try to reduce pollution in a ______________ way.
4. Aber der Smog in der Stuttgarter oder Hamburger Innenstadt ist auch wirklich schlimm.	But the smog in ______________ Stuttgart or Hamburg is really bad too.
5. Die Regierung setzt die Industrie unter Druck, etwas daran zu ändern.	The government has put industries under ______________ to change something.

4 Look at the pictures and complete the sentences.

1. The bottle was under ______________. Now it's broken.
2. The air ______________ is really bad.
3. He got ten ______________ in the test.

5 Find eight words. (↓ and →) Write them in English and German.

E	F	N	D	C	M	E	D	I	A	O
A	N	S	D	R	C	P	O	I	N	T
K	I	B	B	E	X	G	W	Y	P	H
B	R	I	G	A	Q	C	N	F	R	Q
U	J	I	C	T	W	F	T	L	E	D
S	C	A	L	E	S	V	O	Q	S	E
Y	H	A	F	T	F	X	W	A	S	C
D	I	F	F	E	R	E	N	T	U	B
K	O	P	C	U	F	W	Q	I	R	L
R	I	J	L	O	P	A	S	D	E	L

What's the word?

1. Hast du die neuesten Nachrichten auf Jenny Wongs Blog gelesen? — Have you read the ______________ news on Jenny Wong's blog?

2. Jenny ist Expertin für Mode. Sie durchstöbert jeden Tag Geschäfte und Märkte. — Jenny is an expert on fashion. She ______________ shops and markets every day.

3.  — Last week she saw a cool bag in a ________________________ and bought it.

4. Sie schreibt in ihrem Blog auch, wie man mit Mode Geld verdienen kann. — In her blog she also writes about how to ____________________ with fashion.

5. Sie postet immer ein Bild, wenn sie brandneue Kleidung gekauft hat. — She always posts a picture when she has bought __________________ clothes.

6 Put in the right words.

brand-new | browse | downtown | latest | make money | pressure | scale | shop windows

Miss Fashion's trendy blog

Hi everyone!

Can you believe it? I finally found that __________________ bag in Eric Wu's shop. On a _____________ of one to ten I would give it a nine. I was browsing _______ ________________ in Cheung Sha Wan Road in __________________ Hong Kong when I suddenly saw it! It's so hard to find the _____________ clothes if you don't _______________ the shops every day. But don't put yourself under ________________. Shopping must be fun! Next time I'll tell you how to ____________________ by recycling old clothes.

CU soon,

Miss Fashion

What's the word?

1. Normalerweise verkauft Miss Fashion ihre Kleidung wieder, nachdem sie sie nur einmal getragen hat. Dazu hebt sie immer den Originalkarton auf.

   Usually Miss Fashion ______________ her clothes after wearing them only once. That's why she always keeps the ______________ box.

2. Sie liebt den Handel mit Taschen genauso, wie sie zu besitzen.

   She loves ______________ bags as much as owning them.

3. 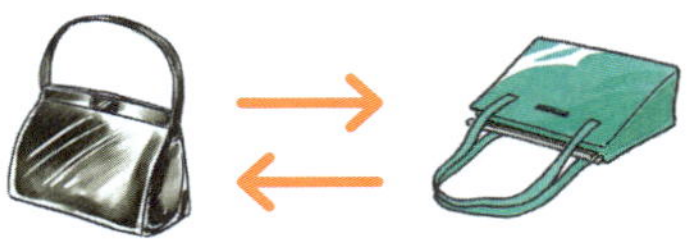

   And she sometimes ______________ bags with her friends.

4. Sie schreibt auch darüber, wie man coole gebrauchte Kleidung findet.

   She also writes about finding cool ______________ clothes.

5. Einige Second-Hand-Läden verkaufen Dinge, die Leute gespendet haben, und geben das Geld dann armen Kindern.

   Some second-hand shops sell things that people ______________ and then give the money to poor children.

6. Man kann seine Stadt kontaktieren, um mehr über das Wiederverkaufen, Tauschen und Spenden von Dingen zu erfahren.

   You can ______________ your town to learn more about reselling, swapping or donating things.

7. Wenn man drei Taschen bei Miss Fashion kauft, erhält man 10 % Rabatt.

   If you buy three bags from Miss Fashion, you will get a 10% ______________.

7 Make sentences. Put the words in the right order.

1. buys • the • fashion. • My • latest • always • sister

   ____

2. best • First • swapped • her • with • she • Jenny. • friend • clothes

   ____

3. things • reselling • began • money. • she • make • Then • to

   ____

4. books • her • to • help • children. • old • clothes • she • and • poor • Sometimes • donates

   ____

8 Complete the words.

A A A A E E E E I I I O O O O O U

1. _ r _ g _ n _ l
2. d _ sc _ _ nt
3. r _ s _ ll
4. d _ n _ t _
5. s _ c _ nd - h _ nd
6. c _ nt _ ct

What's the word?

1. Hast du schon mal von den „Sneakerheads“ gehört?

Have you ever heard about ' sneaker heads '?

2. Ein Sneakerhead kaufte ein Paar Sneaker für 5.000 Hongkong-Dollar. Das sind mehr als 500 Euro.

One sneakerhead bought a pair of sneaker for 5,000 Hong Kong dollars. That's more than 500 euros.

3. Er ist fast ausgeflippt, als er sein Lieblingspaar Goldsneaker gefunden hat.

He almost goes crazy when he found his favourite pair of golden sneakers.

4. Manche Sneakerheads kampieren sogar draußen vor den Läden, um die neuesten und verrücktesten Sneaker zu bekommen.

Some sneakerheads even camp outside the shops to get the latest and craziest sneakers.

5. Henry Fong behauptet, dass er mehr als 1.000 Paar Sneaker besitzt.

Henry Fong claim to own more than 1,000 pairs of sneakers.

6. Ich würde nie mein ganzes Taschengeld für Sneaker ausgeben.

I would never spend all my pocket money on sneakers.

7. Ich habe meine letzten Sneaker mehr als ein Jahr lang jeden Tag getragen.

I wore my last sneakers every day for more than a year.

8. Ich vermute, dass Sneakerheads wie Henry echt reich sind. Die Armen könnten nicht einmal ein Paar teure Sneaker kaufen.

I guess sneakerheads like Henry are really rich. The poor can't even buy one pair of expensive sneakers.

9 Look at the pictures and write the words.

1. Sneaker

2. The poor

3. a pair of jeans

4. to go crazy

5. pocket money

6. to camp

What's the word?

1. Es gibt viele Wege, wie man die Luftverschmutzung verbessern kann.
   There are many ways to ______________ air pollution.
2. Jimmy Jang ist Talkmaster von Hongkongs berühmtester Radioshow, „Grüneres Hongkong".
   Jimmy Jang is the ______________ of Hong Kong's most famous radio show, *Greener Hong Kong*.
3. Er spricht über Verschmutzung und erneuerbare Energie.
   He talks about pollution and ______________ ______________.
4. Experten sagen, dass viele Kraftwerke noch immer Öl und Kohle verwenden, um Strom zu erzeugen.
   Experts say that many ______________ still use oil and coal to produce electricity.
5. Sie arbeiten an neuen Technologien, um saubere Energie zu erzeugen.
   They are working on new ______________ to produce clean energy.
6. Es gibt verschiedene Möglichkeiten, etwas gegen Luftverschmutzung zu unternehmen.
   There are different ______________ to ______________ air pollution.
7. 
   At the moment people wear ______________ to protect themselves.
8. Mit umweltfreundlichen Technologien bräuchten die Leute keine Masken mehr.
   With ______________ technologies people wouldn't need masks any more.
9. Aber es gibt noch andere Probleme. In der Zeitung habe ich gelesen, dass Leute im Alter von 30 bis 45 den Großteil unserer Lebensmittelabfälle produzieren.
   But there are other problems too. I read in the newspaper that people ______________ 30 to 45 produce most of our ______________.

10 Look at the pictures and write the words.

1. ______________
2. ______________
3. ______________

11 Put a circle around the odd one out and write it in German.

1. waste • power plant • mask • improve ______________
2. factories • cars • eco-friendly • planes ______________
3. host • option • nurse • plumber ______________

What's the word?

1. Jimmy gibt auch Tipps, wie man Energie sparen kann. Er sagt, dass man einen Bewegungsmelder verwenden kann, um das Licht einzuschalten.	Jimmy gives tips on how to save energy too. He says you can use a ______________ to turn on your lights.
2. Und man kann Sonnenkollektoren verwenden, um warmes Wasser für die Dusche oder die Badewanne zu erzeugen.	And you can use ______________ to produce hot water for your shower or ______________.
3. Es gibt auch transparente Sonnenkollektoren.	There are also ______________ solar panels.
4. Ein Sonnenkollektor wird aus vielen kleinen Solarzellen hergestellt.	A solar panel is made of many small solar ______________.
5. Wind- und Sonnenenergie produzieren keine Abgase wie Autos.	Wind and solar energy don't produce ______________ like cars.
6. Es gibt viele Entwicklungen bei den erneuerbaren Energien.	There has been a lot of ______________ in renewable energies.
7. Chinesische Experten testen derzeit Gondeln, die die Menschen von einem Ort in der Stadt zu einem anderen bringen.	Chinese experts are testing ______________ that take people from one place of the city to another.
8. 	People can get on and off where they like. The pods look a bit like ______________.

12 Look at the pictures and complete the sentences.

1. You can see through water. It's ______________.
2. Cars produce a lot of ______________.
3. Many homes have ______________ now.

13 Put a circle around the right words.

1. Our eco-friendly car produces very few (electricity • exhaust fumes).
2. (Power plants • Solar panels) need the sun to produce energy.
3. There has been a lot of (development • energy) in new technologies since the 1980s.

What's the word?

1. Die Gondeln, über die Jimmy spricht, fahren über dem Boden.	The pods Jimmy talks about travel ________ the ground.
2. Du kannst zu Hause in eine Gondel einsteigen und sie setzt dich an der Schule ab.	You can get on a pod at home and it ________ you ________ at school.
3. 	The pods have solar panels on their ________.
4. Jimmy behauptete, dass sich die Luftqualität in einigen Gegenden schon verbessert habe.	Jimmy claimed that air ________ had already improved in some areas.
5. 	The pods don't travel on the ground, so ________ and flowers can grow.
6. Das ist nicht nur ein positiver Effekt für die Umwelt, es sieht auch nett aus.	That's not only a positive ________ for the environment, it also looks nice.
7. Jimmy hat Bilder und Diagramme über die Effekte auf seine Webseite gestellt.	Jimmy put pictures and ________ about the effects on his website.
8. Die Diagramme zeigen, dass das Verschmutzungsniveau verringert werden kann, wenn wir mit Solargondeln fahren.	The charts show that pollution ________ can be reduced if we travel by solar pods.

14 Match the words.

1. pollution	a) off
2. drop	b) effect
3. positive	c) quality
4. air	d) levels

15 Complete the two mind maps.

eco-friendly technologies | exhaust fumes | green energy | smog | high pollution levels | power plants | recycling food waste | solar panels

What's the word?

1. Seit der Entwicklung des Internets und der sozialen Medien gibt es viele Fragen darüber, was die Wahrheit ist. — Since the development of the internet and social media there have been a lot of questions about what the ______________ is.

2. Wir können online Informationen über fast alles finden, aber wir wissen nicht immer, ob sie wahr sind oder nicht. — We can find ______________ on almost everything online, but we don't always know if it is true or not.

3. Man kann eine Menge Zeit im Internet verbringen, um die Puzzleteile zu suchen und die Wahrheit herauszufinden. — You can spend a lot of time on the internet looking for the pieces of the ______________ and find out the truth.

4. Die Presse kann Menschen beeinflussen, indem sie zum Beispiel nur Teile der Geschichte erzählt. — The ______________ can influence people by telling only parts of the story, for example.

5. Ein Journalist muss sehr verantwortungsvoll mit den Informationen sein, die er bekommt. — A ______________ must be very responsible with the information he or she gets.

6. In manchen Ländern zensiert die Regierung die Presse. — In some countries the government ______________ the press.

7. Sie kontrolliert die Medien und manchmal werden Journalisten verhaftet oder verschwinden. — It ______________ the media, and sometimes journalists get arrested or disappear.

16 Look at the pictures and write the words.

1. ______________ 2. ______________ 3. ______________

17 Complete the words.

A A E E E E I I I O O O O O O O U U

1. _nf_rm_t__n
2. tr_th
3. j__rn_l_st
4. c_ntr_l
5. c_ns_r
6. d_v_l_pm_nt

What's the word?

1. In einer Demokratie können die Menschen in Wahlen über ihre Regierung abstimmen. — In a ____________ people can vote for their government in elections.
2. Eine Demokratie schützt die Menschenrechte. Das steht in der Verfassung geschrieben. — A democracy protects ____________. This is written in the constitution.
3. Eines dieser Rechte ist die Redefreiheit. — One of those rights is the ____________.
4. Das Gesetz garantiert, dass niemand wegen seiner Meinung verhaftet wird. — The law ____________ that nobody can be arrested for his or her opinion.
5. Aber es gibt Grenzen: Man muss andere Kulturen und Religionen respektieren. — But there are ____________: You must respect other cultures and religions.
6. Auch die Medien sollten objektiv sein und Menschen akzeptieren, die eine andere Meinung haben. — The media should also be ____________ and accept people who have a different opinion.

18 Put in the right words.

censored | contact | controlled | democracy | freedom of speech | had guaranteed | human rights | information | journalist | limits | media | objective | press | truth

The Hong Kong Observer

Hong Kong Mystery

On the night of 17th March 2018 Chow Mai, a young ____________, disappeared from her home in Hong Kong. She is famous for writing the ____________ about ____________ in China. She wrote about her opinion in many ____________ reports. But she knew her ____________ and always tried to be ____________. Friends told the police that Chow Mai had worked on a story about the ____________. She wanted China to become a ____________. She claimed that the government ____________ the ____________ too much. The government ____________ some of her stories. Although it ____________ that she was free to write her opinion, she got some strange phone calls. Now she is gone. If you have some ____________, please ____________ our Hong Kong office at + 852 6852 1233.

What's the word?

1. Mein Vater sagte mir, dass ich kritisch mit Onlineinformationen sein solle.	My dad told me to be ______________ of online information.
2. Wir betrachten Menschenrechte und die Redefreiheit als selbstverständlich.	We ____________ human rights and the freedom of speech ________________.
3. Aber man sollte immer die Quelle der Informationen überprüfen.	But you should always check the ______________ of the information.
4. Wir haben Zugang zu so vielen Informationsquellen, dass es manchmal schwierig ist, zu sagen, was die Wahrheit ist.	We have ______________ to so many sources of information that it is sometimes hard to tell what the truth is.
5. Einschränkungen werden die Leute nicht davon abhalten, nach der Wahrheit zu suchen.	________________ won't keep people from looking for the truth.
6. Einige Onlineinformationen über Hongkong sind lustig, aber nicht wahr. Ich habe gelesen, dass es eine Geschwindigkeitsgrenze für Vögel gibt, aber ich habe das nicht geglaubt.	Some online information about Hong Kong is funny but not true. I read there was a ______________ for birds, but I didn't believe it.
7. Wie viel km/h fliegen Vögel normalerweise?	How fast do those birds usually fly in __________?
8. Na ja, sie fliegen nicht viel in der Stadt. Sie sitzen lieber oben auf den Hochhäusern.	Well, they don't fly a lot in the city. They prefer sitting ________________ the skyscrapers.

19 Look at the pictures and write the words.

1. ________________________ 2. internet ________________ 3. ________________________

20 Put a circle around the right words.

1. People in Europe have (access • way) to different types of media.
2. Most people are not very (critical • objective) of online information.
3. In democratic societies we take human rights for (free • granted).
4. There is a (access • speed limit) for cars in towns.

What's the word?

1. Jim Jam, der einen Modeblog hat, kauft seine Sonnenbrillen in Einkaufszentren und Onlineshops. — Jim Jam, who has a fashion blog, ______________ his sunglasses in malls and online shops.

2. Kleine Läden haben normalerweise nicht viele verschiedene Sonnenbrillen vorrätig. — Small shops usually don't ______________ a lot of different sunglasses.

3. 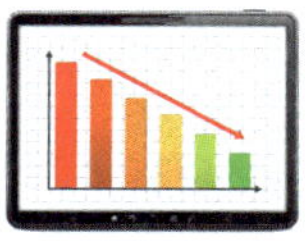 — The number of small shops has ______________ because so many big online shops have opened.

4. Das erzeugt Probleme für die Leute, die in den Läden arbeiten. — This ______________ problems for the people working in the shops.

5. Onlineshops erhöhen manchmal am Abend ihre Preise, weil viele Leute nach der Arbeit das Internet durchstöbern. — Online shops sometimes ______________ their prices in the evening because many people browse the internet after work.

6. Das Onlineeinkaufen hat unser Leben verändert. — Online shopping has ______________ our lives.

7. Einigen Leuten da draußen ist ihr Onlineleben wichtiger als das echte Leben. — There are some people __________ there who think their online life is more important than real life.

21 Make sentences. Put the words in the right order.

1. people • a • purchase • Young • online. • lot

____

2. cities • many • number • shops • In • the • small • decreased. • of • has

____

3. downtown • stock • The • shop • sneakers. • new • doesn't • the

____

4. the • like • to • Teenagers • mall • at • too. • browse • shops

____

22 Put in the right words.

above **for** **of** **of** **to** **under**

1. on top ____________
2. take ____________ granted
3. freedom ____________ speech
4. ____________ the ground
5. ____________ pressure
6. access ____________

What's the word?

1. Zeitungsverleger stellen immer mehr Informationen online. — Newspaper ________________ put more and more information online.

2. Aber das macht es für Regierungen einfacher, die Medien zu kontrollieren und auf die schwarze Liste gesetzte Wörter zu finden. — But this makes it easier for governments to control the media and find ________________ words.

3. Es ist ein Zeichen der Unterdrückung, wenn eine Regierung die Medien zensiert. — It is a sign of ________________ when a government censors the media.

4. Aber es muss auch etwas Kontrolle geben, um zu gewährleisten, dass die Leute keine Gewalt verherrlichen. — But there must be some control to guarantee that people do not ________________ violence.

5. In vielen Ländern findet man rechtsorientierte Kommentare im Internet. — You can find ________________ comments on the internet in many countries.

6. Jede Art von Extremismus ist schlecht. Wir sollten uns gegenseitig respektieren und andere Kulturen tolerieren. — Every type of ________________ is bad. We should respect each other and tolerate different cultures.

23 Match the opposites. ↔

1. censor
2. purchase
3. oppression
4. publisher
5. increase

a) sell
b) reader
c) decrease
d) let people say and write what they want
e) freedom

24 Complete the crossword.

Down ▼:

1. when there is no freedom of speech

Across ▶:

2. say that something is really good
3. when people glorify violence and have very strong opinions
4. the person who owns a newspaper
5. Germany is a free country. It's a …

Blue Line 5

Vokabeltraining aktiv

Lösungsheft

V

Klett

What's the word?

1. Meine Damen und Herren, ich werde Sie auf eine Reise mitnehmen. — Ladies and gentlemen, I'm going to take you on a trip.
2. Wir werden Australien erkunden. — We're going to explore Australia.
3. Das ist ein toller Kontinent. — It's a great continent.
4. Einst war er Teil der Antarktis. — Once it was part of Antarctica.
5. Der australische Kontinent ist zwanzig Mal so groß wie Deutschland. — The Australian continent is twenty times the size of Germany.
6. Die Australier sind sehr lockere Menschen. — Australians are very easy-going people.
7. An der Ostküste gibt es interessante Tiere. — There are interesting animals on the east coast.
8.  — Just think of the koala.
9.  — My favourite animal is the kangaroo.

1 Put in the right words.

continent | easy-going | explore | kangaroos | koala | Ladies and gentlemen

1. Ladies and gentlemen, welcome to Australia. People here are very relaxed. Australia is an easy-going country.
2. Together we're going to explore the continent.
3. I'm going to show you some funny animals like the koala.
4. We're also going to see some kangaroos, of course.

What's the word?

1. Die meisten Touristen lieben Australien. — Most tourists love Australia.
2. Sie mögen die spektakulären Aussichten. — They like the spectacular views.
3. Sie mögen auch all die ungewöhnlichen Tiere. — They also like all the unusual animals.
4. Die meisten Arten gibt es nur auf diesem Kontinent. — Most species can only be found on this continent.
5. Deshalb ist Australien auch als guter Ort zum Tiere-Beobachten bekannt. — That is why Australia is known as a good place to see animals.

2 Find the words. Write them in English and German.

spectacularspeciesunusualmostexplorecontinent

spectacular – spektakulär
species – Art; Spezies
unusual – ungewöhnlich; außergewöhnlich
most – die meisten; die Mehrheit
explore – erkunden; erforschen
continent – Kontinent; Erdteil

3 Put a circle around the right words.

1. Not everyone likes koalas, but (few • most) people do.
2. She looks strange. Her hair is (nice • unusual).
3. The view is (big • spectacular). Look, the mountain is so huge!
4. There are many unusual (types • species) in Australia.

4 Match the words with the same meaning.

1. special
2. fantastic
3. almost all
4. relaxed
5. go out and have a look

a) spectacular
b) explore
c) unusual
d) most
e) easy-going

What's the word?

1. Die Aborigines leben seit mehr als 50.000 Jahren in Australien. — The Aboriginal people have lived in Australia for over 50,000 years.
2. Die Zuwanderung von Europäern nach Australien begann Ende des 18. Jahrhunderts. — The immigration of Europeans to Australia started at the end of the 18th century.
3. Als europäische Siedler nach Australien kamen, verloren viele Aborigines die Kontrolle über ihr Land. — When European settlers came to Australia, many Aboriginal people lost control over their land.
4. 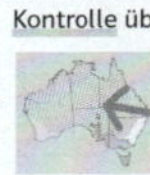 — Aboriginal people used to live in the outback. Today most of them live in cities.
5. Manche Aborigine-Kinder gehen aufs Internat. — Some Aboriginal children go to boarding school.
6. Wenn sie mit der Schule fertig sind, können sie qualifizierte Jobs bekommen. — When they finish school, they can get skilled jobs.
7.  — Some are carpenters.
8. Viele Frauen sind Krankenschwestern. — Many women are nurses.

5 Look at the picture and write the words.

1. Australian continent
2. koala
3. kangaroo
4. Aboriginal woman
5. nurse
6. the outback

What's the word?

1. Wegen der großen Entfernungen haben die Kinder im Outback Mühe, in die Stadt zu kommen. — Children in the outback *struggle* to get to town because of the long distances.
2. Sie können nicht wie andere Kinder die Schule besuchen. — They cannot *attend* school like other children.
3.  — They use a *satellite dish* to watch lessons on TV.
4. Sie treffen ihre Lehrer nur dreimal im Semester. — They only meet their teachers three times a *term*.
5. Sie freuen sich darauf, sie zu sehen. — They *look forward to* seeing them.

6 Put in the right words.

attend | Australia | boarding school | explore | look forward to | most | nurse | satellite dish | struggle | term | the outback | unusual

E-MAIL

Hi Sam,

Thanks for your e-mail. You wanted to know a bit about my life in *Australia*. Well, my family and I live in *the outback*. That's a large area in the centre of Australia. The big cities are far away. That's why I can't *attend* a regular school, and my brothers and sisters can't either. We have a *satellite dish* and watch lessons on the TV instead. That's very cool. But it's not always easy to study at home. Sometimes we *struggle* to do all our homework and stay motivated without help from the teachers. My cousin Adina goes to a *boarding school* in Melbourne. She is hard-working and wants to be a *nurse*. At the end of the *term* she usually comes to visit us and we spend *most* of our time outside. Australia has many *unusual* animals. So there's a lot to *explore*. I always *look forward to* seeing Adina because she has so many interesting stories from school to tell. ☺

Love,

Jindalee

What's the word?

1. Man darf nicht respektlos gegenüber der Kultur der Aborigines sein. — You mustn't be *disrespectful* of Aboriginal culture.
2. Es ist nicht akzeptabel, Witze über ihre Kultur zu machen. — It is not *acceptable* to make jokes about their culture.
3. Es ist nicht in Ordnung, ihre Traditionen zu ignorieren. — It is not OK to *ignore* their traditions.
4. Einige Touristen sind echt ignorant. Sie werfen zum Beispiel ihren Abfall auf die Straße. — Some tourists are really *ignorant*. They throw their rubbish on the street, for example.
5. Wir alle sollten mehr Toleranz für das Leben anderer zeigen. — We all should show more *tolerance* for other people's lives.
6. „Ignorieren" ist ein Verb. — 'To ignore' is a *verb*.

7 Put a circle around the right words.

1. There are so many English ((verbs) • species) to learn.
2. Pushing people on the bus is not ((acceptable) • skilled).
3. People who don't respect other cultures are (easy-going • (ignorant)).
4. You mustn't be ((disrespectful) • unusual) when you visit a foreign country.
5. Please don't (ignorant • (ignore)) me! I would like to talk to you.

8 Make sentences. Put the words in the right order.

1. class • in • is • Shouting • acceptable. • not
   Shouting in class is not acceptable.
2. the • test. • I • all • knew • the • verbs • in
   I knew all the verbs in the test.
3. to • survive • Kangaroos • in • water. • the outback • without • struggle
   Kangaroos struggle to survive in the outback without water.
4. understand • I • John • don't • is • ignoring • why • me.
   I don't understand why John is ignoring me.

What's the word?

1. Die meisten Erwachsenen haben zu Hause Höflichkeit gelernt. — Most adults learnt *politeness* at home.
2. Ihre Eltern tolerierten keine Unverschämtheit. — Their parents did not tolerate *rudeness*.
3. Meine Oma sagt, dass junge Leute oft Respektlosigkeit zeigen. — My grandma says young people often show *disrespect*.
4. Sie gehört zu einer älteren Generation und war nicht auf der Universität. — She belongs to an older *generation* and did not go to *university*.
5. Junge Menschen haben ihre eigenen Überzeugungen. — Young people have their own *beliefs*.
6. Aber meine Oma denkt, sie sind unhöflich. — But my gandma thinks they are *rude*.

9 Look at the pictures and complete the sentences.

1. My grandpa belongs to an older *generation*. But he is really cool.

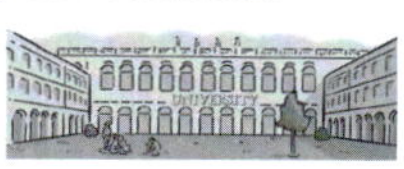

2. When many young people finish school, they go to *university*.

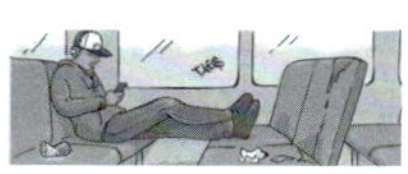

3. I don't like some teenagers' *disrespect* for the rules.

10 Match the opposites. ⟷

1. politeness — c) rudeness
2. east — a) west
3. term — b) holidays
4. ignore — e) respect
5. regular — d) unusual

11 Complete the words.

A A A E E E E E E E E E E I I I I I O O U U

1. b*e*l*i**e*f
2. *a*cc*e*pt*a*bl*e*
3. r*u*d*e*
4. *u*n*i*v*e*rs*i*ty
5. p*o*l*i*t*e*n*e*ss
6. g*e*n*e*r*a*t*i*o*n*

What's the word?

1. Der Uluru ist ein heiliger Ort für die Aborigines. — Uluru is a *sacred* place to the Aboriginal people.
2. Vor langer Zeit lebten dort riesige Kreaturen. — Giant *creatures* lived there a long time ago.
3. Deshalb hat der Uluru eine besondere Bedeutung für die Aborigines. — That is why Uluru has a special *meaning* to the Aboriginal people.
4. Du kannst den Uluru nur mit einem Reiseleiter besichtigen. — You can only go to Uluru with a *guide*.
5. Die Reiseleiter werden dich herumführen. — The guides will *show you around*.
6. Sie erlauben kein anstößiges Verhalten. — They don't allow *offensive* *behaviour*.
7. Hier ist die Bewerbung für Besucher. Du musst sie unterschreiben und einschicken. — Here is the *application* for visitors. You have to sign it and *send* it *in*.

12 Look at the pictures and complete the sentences.

1. Hi. I'm Sam. I'm your *guide*. I'll *show you around* the city.

2. Uluru is a *sacred* place with a special *meaning*.

3. Welcome to the job. I'm glad your *application* was successful.

4. When you visit Uluru, offensive *behaviour* is not allowed.

5. I'll *send in* my application today.

6. Please sign this *application* for visitors.

What's the word?

1. Einige Aborigine-Stämme leben in der Nähe des Uluru. — Some Aboriginal tribes live near Uluru.
2. Der Uluru ist ein überwältigender Ort. — Uluru is a stunning place.
3. Jeden Morgen heißen die Stämme die Sonne willkommen. — Each morning the tribes welcome the sun.
4.  — Then they take the path to their sacred rock.
5. Man kann bei dieser Tradition zuschauen, aber man muss leise sein und die Regeln respektieren. — You can watch this tradition, but you need to be quiet and respect the rules.

13 Put the words in the right group.

boarding school · carpenter · disrespectful · guide · ignorant · kangaroo · nurse · path · rude · term · the outback · university

jobs	nature	behaviour	school and education
carpenter	kangaroo	disrespectful	boarding school
guide	path	ignorant	term
nurse	the outback	rude	university

14 Put in the right words.

behaviour · beliefs · creatures · disrespectful · ignorant · meaning · need to · sacred · stunning

Many children in Germany are ignorant of their traditions. Their parents don't tell them sacred stories any more. If you don't know these stunning stories, it's difficult to understand the meaning of our traditions. Traditions tell us what good behaviour is. For example, we mustn't be disrespectful of other people or creatures and we need to respect other people's beliefs.

What's the word?

1.  — My friend used to be a bike courier in Sydney.
2. Dafür brauchte sie keine besonderen Fähigkeiten. — She didn't need any special skills for that.
3. Sie hatte keine Berufserfahrung. — She didn't have any work experience.
4. Aber sie ist immer pünktlich. — But she is always punctual.
5. Jetzt arbeitet sie als Reisebürokauffrau. — Now she works as a travel agent.
6. Sie ist effizient und fleißig. — She is efficient and hard-working.
7. Sie bucht normalerweise Reisen, aber manchmal arbeitet sie auch in der Verwaltung oder im Kundendienst. — She usually books holidays, but she sometimes works in the administration department or customer service too.
8. Sie ist froh, dass sie einen unbefristeten Job hat. — She is happy to have a permanent job.

15 Put a circle around the odd one out and write it in German.

1. nurse • travel agent • bike courier • (work experience) Berufserfahrung
2. skilled • (administration) • punctual • efficient Verwaltung
3. tired • slow • late • (punctual) pünktlich

16 Find seven words. (↓ and →) Write them in English and German.

B	I	K	E	C	O	U	R	I	E	R	T
P	Z	U	I	O	P	X	C	A	Q	Y	R
E	I	R	S	K	I	L	L	S	K	L	A
R	B	R	Y	Q	W	E	R	S	F	G	V
M	E	X	A	F	F	I	L	U	C	E	E
A	P	U	N	C	T	U	A	L	R	E	L
N	N	T	P	Y	H	E	S	T	M	B	A
E	H	P	O	T	R	A	L	Z	I	N	G
N	E	F	F	I	C	I	E	N	T	A	E
T	A	P	P	L	I	C	A	T	I	O	N
X	Z	S	H	I	M	S	R	Y	D	F	T

bike courier – Fahrradkurier; Fahrradkurierin
skills – Fähigkeiten
punctual – pünktlich
efficient – effizient; leistungsfähig
application – Bewerbung
permanent – unbefristet; dauerhaft; permanent
travel agent – Reiseverkehrskaufmann; Reiseverkehrskauffrau

What's the word?

1. Ich sah eine Anzeige für einen Elektriker. — I saw an advert for an electrician.
2. Die Firma sucht einen Muttersprachler. — The company is looking for a native speaker.
3. Das Gehalt, das sie bieten, ist gut. — The salary they offer is good.
4.  — They want to see a certificate.
5. Sie benötigen auch zwei Referenzschreiben. — They also need two references.
6. Ich rief die Empfangschefin der Firma an. — I phoned the receptionist at the company.
7. Sie sagte mir, ich solle einen Bewerbungsbrief schreiben. — She told me to write a letter of application.
8. Ich schickte eine E-Mail und schrieb: „Angefügt erhalten Sie meinen Lebenslauf." — I sent an e-mail and wrote 'Please find attached my CV.'

17 Look at the pictures and complete the sentences.

1. receptionist

2. electrician

3. letter of application

18 Say the words. Then complete the table.

application · certificate · certificate · CV · electrician · electrician · receptionist · references

sounds like a German 'k'	sounds like a German 'ß'	sounds like a German 'sch'
application	certificate	electrician
certificate	CV	
electrician	receptionist	
	references	

What's the word?

1. Ich möchte für eine chinesische Firma arbeiten. — I want to work for a Chinese company.
2. Die Firma ist in Hongkong, auf einer Insel nahe der chinesischen Küste. — The company is in Hong Kong on an island near the Chinese coast.
3. Der Job ist im Kundenservice. Also brauche ich gute Kommunikationsfähigkeiten. — The job is in customer service so I need good communication skills.
4. Ich schrieb ein Motivationsschreiben und erzählte ihnen von meinen Interessen. — I wrote a personal statement and told them about my interests.
5. Ich musste Details und die Rechtschreibung beachten. — I had to pay attention to detail and to my spelling.
6. Ich schrieb auch einen Bewerbungsbrief. Ich beendete den Brief mit „Mit freundlichen Grüßen". — I also wrote a letter of application. I ended the letter with 'Yours sincerely,'.

19 Complete the dialogue.

attached · certificates · Chinese · efficient · interests · offer · pay attention · personal statement · work experience

1 I've read your CV, but I can't see your personal statement.

2 Oh, I thought it was attached to the e-mail.

3 Oh, yes. Here it is.

4 I also sent you my school certificates.

5 Good. I can see you're efficient. You also pay attention to detail and have many interests.

6 Thank you.

7 Your work experience looks very good. It seems you have a lot to offer. But do you really want to work in China?

8 Oh, yes. I love Chinese culture! And I speak some Chinese.

What's the word?

1. Der Klimawandel ist für die Welt ein Problem. — Climate change is a problem for the world.
2. Er ist eine große Gefahr für das Great Barrier Reef. — It is a big danger to the Great Barrier Reef.
3.  — The coral is a very special animal.
4. Die Koralle ist Teil der Unterwasserwelt und sieht aus wie ein Riff aus Stein. — The coral is part of the underwater world and looks like a reef made of stone.
5. Manche Leute sagen, sie sei ein Unterwasserwunder. — Some people say it is an underwater wonder.
6. Sich verändernde Wassertemperaturen sind nicht gut für die Korallen. — Changing water temperatures are not good for the coral.
7. Veränderungen in der Umwelt verursachen den Tod der Korallen und anderer Unterwasserlebewesen. — Changes in the environment cause the death of the coral and other underwater creatures.

20 Match the questions and the answers.

1. Are you worried about the weather?
2. Do you think Tom will be safe?
3. What do you want to do in Australia?
4. What causes the death of the coral?
5. Is there a problem with the reefs?

a) I want to see the underwater reefs.
b) Changes in the environment.
c) Yes, he will. There's no danger.
d) Yes, the changing temperatures are bad for them.
e) No, I'm worried about climate change.

21 Find the words. Write them in English and German.

temperaturewonderdeathreefdangerenvironment

temperature – Temperatur
wonder – Wunder
death – Tod; Todesfall
reef – Riff
danger – Gefahr
environment – Umwelt; Umgebung

What's the word?

1.  — I was on holiday in Sicily.
2.  — I sat down on the beach and watched the moon.
3. Ich hörte auch den Geräuschen des großen weiten Meeres zu. — I also listened to the sound of the wide open sea.
4. Aber der Strand war voller Vogelexkremente. — But the beach was full of bird waste.
5. Die Exkremente riechen schlecht und verursachen Schaden an den Bäumen. — The waste smells bad and it causes damage to the trees.
6. Die Regierung will das stoppen. — The government wants to stop this.
7. Sie haben sich auf ein Programm geeinigt, einige Vögel in den Zoo zu bringen. — They have agreed on a programme to take some of the birds to a zoo.
8. Ich finde es gut, wenn sich die Menschen für die Umwelt interessieren. — I think it's good when people care about the environment.

22 What is it? Write the word.

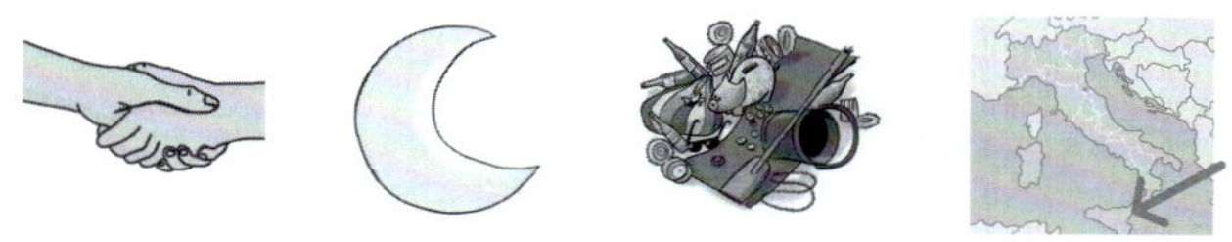

1. You can see it when it is dark, but it is not a star. moon
2. It is an island in Italy. Sicily
3. things people throw away waste
4. When you have the same idea, you agree on an idea.

23 Find the words that rhyme.

belief | care | CV | moon | wide | wonder

1. TV – CV
2. wear – care
3. reef – belief
4. side – wide
5. soon – moon
6. under – wonder

What's the word?

1.  — The waste in the oceans is bad for whales.
2.  — It's also a problem for turtles.
3. Walhaie und tropische Fische fressen den Müll und sterben. — Whale sharks and tropical fish eat the waste and die.
4. Auch die Delfine und Teufelsrochen sind in Gefahr. — Dolphins and manta rays are in danger too.
5. Die Salzwasserkrokodile leben nicht in dieser Gegend und fressen den Müll deshalb nicht. — Saltwater crocodiles don't live in that area so they won't eat the waste.

24 Put the words in the right order.

1. waste • The • from • ship • killed • whale sharks. • the • many
   The waste from the ship killed many whale sharks.
2. many • the • Australia • has • manta ray. • interesting • animals • like
   Australia has many interesting animals like the manta ray.
3. and • live • the • in • Great Barrier Reef. • Turtles • fish • also • tropical
   Turtles and tropical fish also live in the Great Barrier Reef.

25 Right or wrong?

	right	wrong
1. Turtles live in the ocean.	✓	
2. The manta ray is a species of fish.	✓	
3. Saltwater crocodiles can't survive in the ocean.		✓
4. Waste is a danger for fish and birds.	✓	
5. Whale sharks are very small.		✓

What's the word?

1.  — Scientists often get good jobs.
2. Sie studieren Chemikalien oder Algen. — They study chemicals or algae.
3. Wissenschaftliche Jobs ziehen oft Jungen an. — Science jobs often attract boys.
4. Einige Jungen wollen Physiotherapeuten werden. — Some boys want to become physiotherapists.
5. Physiotherapeuten müssen respektvoll und tolerant sein, denn sie arbeiten mit Menschen. — Psychotherapists have to be respectful and tolerant because they work with people.
6. Einige Mädchen möchten Klempnerinnen werden. — Some girls want to become plumbers.
7. Andere möchten als Telefonistinnen für große Firmen arbeiten. — Others want to work as telephonists for big companies.
8. Aber ich glaube, niemand möchte in einem Callcenter arbeiten, denn oft zeigen die Leute, die man anruft, keinen Respekt. — But I think nobody wants to work in a call centre because the people you call often don't show respect.

26 Look at the pictures and write the words.

1. plumber
2. receptionist
3. physiotherapist

27 Complete the words.

-able | -al | -ance | -ant | -ful | -ive | -ness | -ness

1. respectful
2. politeness
3. acceptable
4. tolerance
5. rudeness
6. tolerant
7. offensive
8. tropical

What's the word?

1. Tropische Stürme kommen zur Regenzeit. — Tropical storms come in the *rainy season*.
2. Sie führen zu Problemen für alle. — They *result in* problems for everyone.
3.  — That is why tourists go *snorkelling* during the summer.
4. Dann sind die Schnorchelplattformen sicher. — Then the snorkelling *platforms* are safe.
5. Das Ausbleichen durch Sonnenlicht kann ein Problem für die Plattformen sein. — Sun *bleaching* can be a problem for the platforms.
6. Das Holz erholt sich nicht davon. Es verliert seine Farbe und sieht nicht mehr schön aus. — The wood won't *recover* from it. It loses its colour and doesn't look nice any more.

28 Look at the pictures and complete the sentences.

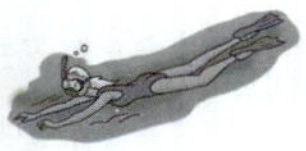

1. There are many storms in the *rainy season*.
2. She loves *snorkelling*.
3. Will the ocean's *recover* from all the waste?

29 Put in the right words.

algae | bleaching | chemicals | coral | creatures | danger | rainy season | Reef | results in | snorkelling | will recover

E-MAIL

Hi Dad,

I just visited the Great Barrier *Reef* and went *snorkelling*. The *coral* is so beautiful! Coral *bleaching*, however, is a *danger* to the reef. It *results in* the death of the *algae* on the coral. When the algae die, the underwater *creatures* lose their food. The *rainy season* is a problem too because the rain carries *chemicals* into the ocean. I'm not sure if the sea *will recover* from it.

Love,

Liz

What's the word?

1.  — *Oil spills* are a problem for the environment.
2. Sie können sich bis über hundert Meilen erstrecken. — They can *stretch* across more than hundred miles.
3. Sie verschmutzen die Ozeane. — They *pollute* the oceans.
4. Sie sind auch gefährlich für die Schiffe, die vorbeikommen. — They are also dangerous for the ships that *pass*.
5. Der Zustand der Strände ist auch schrecklich. — The beaches are in a terrible *state* too.
6. Die Ignoranz der Ölfirmen ist Teil dieses Problems. — The *ignorance* of the oil companies is part of the problem.
7. Es gibt nicht mehr viel Akzeptanz für Ölfirmen. — There's not much *acceptance* for oil companies any more.

30 Put in the right words.

death | oil spills | pollute | recover | species | state | stretch

We hear about *oil spills* almost every month. They often *stretch* across hundreds of miles. They *pollute* the water and the beaches and cause the *death* of many underwater *species* and birds. This is not an acceptable *state* for the wildlife. If oil spills happen again and again, the oceans will not *recover* from them.

31 Complete the mind map.

algae | chemicals | changing temperatures | coral | coral bleaching | dolphins | more tropical storms | oil spills | death of species | waste | whales

the environment

- climate change: *changing temperatures*, *more tropical storms*, *death of species*
- other dangers: *oil spills*, *chemicals*, *waste*
- plants and animals: *coral*, *dolphins*, *algae*, *whales*

What's the word?

1. Viele Leute machen in der Karibik Urlaub. — Many people go on holiday to *the Caribbean*.
2. Die sandigen Strände sind sehr beliebt. — The *sandy* beaches are very popular.
3. Alle karibischen Inseln haben Hotels. — All *Caribbean* islands have hotels.
4. Im Herbst kommen wenige Touristen. — Few tourists come in the *autumn*.
5.  — It is *hurricane* season.

1 Look at the pictures and complete the sentences.

1. Many tourists go on holiday to the *Caribbean* in the winter.
2. The worst time to go is in the *autumn* because it is *hurricane* season.
3. Tourists love the *sandy* beaches.

2 Match the words.

1. sandy
2. hurricane
3. autumn
4. Caribbean

a) storms
b) beaches
c) islands
d) season

3 Find the words. Write them in English and German.

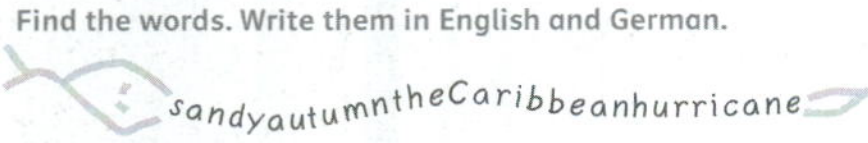

sandy – sandig
autumn – Herbst
the Caribbean – die Karibik
hurricane – Wirbelsturm; Orkan

What's the word?

1. Die karibischen Inseln waren früher Kolonien. — The Caribbean islands used to be *colonies*.
2. Manche Inseln waren niederländische Kolonien. — Some islands were *Dutch* colonies.
3. Andere gehörten den Briten. — Others belonged to *the British*.
4. Viele Kariben sind gute Musiker. — Many Caribbean people are good *musicians*.
5. Sie lieben schnelle Rhythmen. — They love quick *rhythms*.
6. Sie schreiben ihre eigenen Liedtexte. — They write their own *lyrics*.
7. Bob Marley ist ihr Vorbild. — Bob Marley is their *role model*.
8. Ihr Ziel ist es, so berühmt zu werden wie er. — Their *goal* is to become famous like him.
9. Zur Zeit gibt es eine Rückkehr von Musik aus den 80ern und 90ern. — There has been a *return* to music from the '80s and '90s.

4 Look at the pictures and complete the sentences.

1. Jamaica is one of the *Caribbean* islands.
2. Some islands were *Dutch* colonies.
3. Other islands were Spanish *colonies*.

4. *The British* came to the Caribbean in the 17th century.
5. Look, the football player is near the *goal*!
6. I want to become a famous *musician* one day.

What's the word?

1. Meine Eltern und ich waren in den Ferien auf den Bahamas. — My parents and I went on holiday to the Bahamas.
2. Wir fuhren mit der Fähre dorthin. — We went there by ferry.
3. Die Fähre fuhr ohne Verspätung ab. — The ferry left without delay.
4. Meine Eltern hatten ein Luxusresort gebucht. — My parents had booked a luxury resort.
5. Mir gefiel die Unterkunft. — I loved the accommodation.
6. Ich werde nie wieder in einer normalen Ferienanlage übernachten. — I will never stay in a regular resort again.
7. Meine Schwester mag dennoch lieber Couchsurfing. — But my sister still prefers couch surfing.

5 Complete the dialogue.

accommodation · the Bahamas · Caribbean · couch surfing · hurricane · luxury resort · musicians · where · why

1. How was your holiday in the Caribbean?
2. Awesome! We stayed in a luxury resort.
3. Where was the resort?
4. It was in the Bahamas.
5. What did you like most?
6. I loved the Caribbean musicians. And our hotel was so much better than couch surfing. But I was afraid to leave our accommodation in the dark.
7. Why was that?
8. I thought a hurricane was on its way.

What's the word?

1. Meine Freunde buchten ein Zimmer in einem Hotel in Trinidad. — My friends booked a room at a hotel in Trinidad.
2. Sie wollten Inselhopping machen. — They wanted to do some island hopping.
3.  — They took their passports with them on the ferry.
4. Sie mussten sie am Gate zeigen. — They had to show them at the gate.
5. Dann durften sie an Bord der Fähre gehen. — Then they were allowed to board the ferry.
6. Sie liebten die Schönheit der Karibik. — They loved the beauty of the Caribbean.
7. Sie raubte ihnen den Atem. — It took their breath away.

6 Choose the right word.

beauty · board · delay · ferry · passport · Trinidad

1. bus • plane • ferry
2. enter • go in • board
3. Jamaica • Bahamas • Trinidad
4. early • on time • delay
5. gate • ticket • passport
6. woman • pretty • beauty

7 Match the sentence parts.

1. We'll spend our holiday
2. We'll take the ferry
3. We can board
4. But there is a delay
5. I'm glad we can still
6. I'm looking forward

a) because it's cheap.
b) do some island hopping.
c) because of a storm.
d) in Trinidad.
e) to the beauty of the place.
f) at two in the afternoon.

What's the word?

1. Die Britischen Jungferninseln sind für Wassersport berühmt. — The British Virgin Islands are famous for water sports.
2.  — Diving is very popular there.
3. Am Strand gibt es Tauchschulen. — There are diving schools on the beach.
4. Man kann unter Wasser Schiffswracks sehen. — You can see shipwrecks under the water.
5. Es ist eine außergewöhnliche Erfahrung. — It is an extraordinary experience.
6. Unser Hostel bietet auch Tauchstunden an. — Our hostel offers diving lessons too.
7. Sie finden jeden Tag statt. — They take place every day.

8 Look at the pictures and complete the sentences.

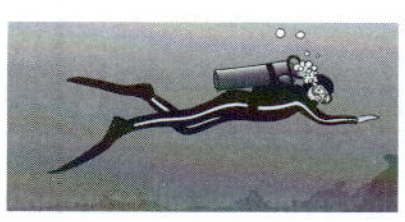

1. The Caribbean is famous for diving.
2. There are many diving schools on the islands.
3. Many people go to the British Virgin Islands to go diving.

4. There are many hostels in the Caribbean.
5. Surfing lessons take place every day.
6. Tourists also want to see the shipwrecks.

9 Find the words that rhyme.

delay · ferry · gate · goal · return · sandy

1. learn – return
2. Mandy – sandy
3. pay – delay
4. hole – goal
5. late – gate
6. Jerry – ferry

What's the word?

1.  — The Caribbean is also famous for its volcanoes.
2. Ein entfernter Vulkan ist für Touristen nicht gefährlich. — A distant volcano is not dangerous for tourists.
3.  — Sometimes you can see lightning behind them.
4. Man kann auch den Donner hören. — You can hear thunder too.
5. Wenn kein Sturm in der Nähe ist, können sich die Menschen am Strand entspannen. — When there is no storm nearby, people can relax on the beach.
6. Einige Touristen feiern den ganzen Tag und essen Meeresfrüchte am Strand. — Some tourists party all day and eat seafood on the beach.

10 Put a circle around the odd one out and write it in German.

1. ship • (volcano) • ferry • boat — Vulkan
2. thunder • lightning • (seafood) • storm — Meeresfrüchte
3. work • study • (relax) • clean — sich entspannen; sich ausruhen

11 Look at the picture and complete the sentences.

Sue and Peter want to find seafood (1) today. It's hot on the sandy (2) beach. But there is a storm nearby. Peter does not like the sound of thunder (3). Sue is worried about the lightning (4). Maybe they should go home.

What's the word?

1. Meine Eltern sind ziemlich konservativ. — My parents are quite conservative.
2. Ihnen ist Religion sehr wichtig. — Religion is very important to them.
3. Sie haben einen starken Glauben. — Their faith is strong.
4. Sie haben hart dafür gearbeitet, um in die Gesellschaft hineinzupassen. — They worked hard to fit in.
5. Als mein Bruder 16 war, hat er sich als schwul geoutet. — When my brother was 16, he came out as gay.
6.  — It was a shock to the whole family when he told them.
7. Sie wollten nie auffallen. — They never wanted to stand out.
8. Aber ihre Werte helfen ihnen, locker zu sein. — But their values help them to be easy-going.
9. Jetzt sprechen sie überall darüber. — Now they talk about it everywhere.
10. Sie sind nicht so altmodisch, wie ich dachte. — They are not as old-fashioned as I thought.

12 Find nine words. (↓ and →) Write them in English and German.

S	V	A	L	U	E	S	W	E	O	R
F	T	Z	W	S	O	P	A	S	L	D
A	F	G	X	T	S	T	A	N	D	H
I	J	K	A	A	X	C	V	B	-	N
T	P	O	L	N	R	E	W	Q	F	A
H	F	D	T	D	H	J	K	G	A	Y
E	I	S	H	O	C	K	T	U	S	E
C	T	X	C	U	B	N	M	Q	H	W
K	I	R	T	T	U	I	O	P	I	A
S	N	F	R	E	L	I	G	I	O	N
R	N	S	P	E	C	T	G	H	N	K
E	V	E	R	Y	W	H	E	R	E	N
S	V	I	M	L	O	R	C	H	D	S

values – Werte; Wertvorstellungen
gay – schwul; homosexuell
shock – Schock
religion – Religion
everywhere – überall
faith – Glaube
fit in – hineinpassen
stand out – auffallen
old-fashioned – altmodisch

What's the word?

1. Gestern Abend surfte Lisa im Internet. — Last night Lisa surfed the internet.
2. Sie glaubt an Freundschaft im Internet. — She believes in internet friendship.
3. Ich denke, Onlinefreundschaften sind kompliziert. — I think online friendships are complicated.
4. Man weiß nicht, ob man auf die Dinge, die die Leute online schreiben, vertrauen kann. — You don't know if you can rely on the things people write online.
5. Es ist eine Anstrengung, online den richtigen Mann oder die richtige Frau zu finden. — It's a struggle to find the right man or woman online.
6. Aber die Zahl der Leute, die ihren Partner im Internet finden, steigt an. — But the number of people who find their partner on the internet is growing.
7.  — Many people marry a person they've met online.

13 Put in the right words.

complicated | conservative | friendship | gay | last night | relax | rely on | shock | values

E-MAIL

Dear Sue,

Thanks for your message. I saw it last night. I hope this isn't a shock for you, but I'm gay. I'm only looking for friendship. You say you aren't conservative, and I think you have good values. So being friends won't be too complicated, will it? You can trust me and rely on me as a friend. Now that I told you, I hope we can relax.

Please write to me soon.

Love, Phil

14 Match the opposites. ↔

1. relax
2. modern
3. fit in
4. easy
5. boring

a) old-fashioned
b) extraordinary
c) complicated
d) be nervous
e) stand out

What's the word?

1. 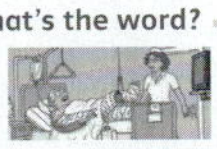 — Susan wants to study nursing when she finishes school.
2. Sie möchte unabhängig sein und ihr eigenes Geld verdienen. — She wants to be independent and earn her own money.
3. Sie schrieb in den sozialen Medien über ihre Pläne. Viele Leute kommentierten dies. — She wrote about her plans on social media. Many people commented on it.
4. Es gab eine interessante Aussage. — There was an interesting statement.
5. Jemand sagte, es gebe nicht genügend Krankenschwestern und dies sei ein ständiges Problem. — Someone said there weren't enough nurses and that it was a constant problem.
6. Ich denke, er hat recht. Einerseits gibt es so viele alte Menschen, die Krankenpflege brauchen. — I think he's right. On the one hand, there are so many old people who need nursing.
7. Andererseits verdienen Krankenpfleger nicht viel Geld. Deshalb wollen nur wenige Leute den Job machen. — On the other hand, nurses don't earn a lot of money, so very few people want to do the job.

15 Put in the right words.

complicated | independent | nursing | on the one hand | on the other hand

Hi. You said that something was complicated?
Yes. My grandpa isn't well.

What's wrong with him?

He isn't independent any more.

Oh, no! What happened?

He needs to go into a nursing home.

Doesn't he want to go?

Well, on the one hand, he can't pay for it. On the other hand, he needs constant nursing.

What's the word?

1. Es gibt viel Gewalt in Sams Straße. — There is a lot of violence in Sam's street.
2. Sein Vater starb in einer Schießerei. — His dad died in a shooting.
3. 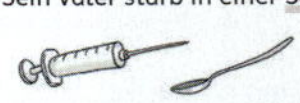 — His brother takes drugs.
4. Er hat Angst, dass bald wieder Gewalt ausbrechen könnte. — He is afraid violence could break out again soon.
5. Obwohl Sam an Freundschaft glaubt, ist sein Leben schwer. — Although Sam believes in friendship, his life is hard.
6. Sam geht gern zur Schule. Er weiß, dass es ein Privileg ist. Andere Jungen in seiner Straße müssen stattdessen arbeiten gehen. — Sam likes going to school. He knows it's a privilege. Other boys in his street have to work instead.

16 Match the sentences with the picture.

The family is happy although they are poor. | The tourists have many privileges. | They are selling drugs. | They don't like violence. | He listens to music everywhere. | He was hurt in a shooting.

1. The family is happy although they are poor.
2. They don't like violence.
3. He listens to music everywhere.
4. They are selling drugs.
5. He was hurt in a shooting.
6. The tourists have many privileges.

What's the word?

1. Barbados ist in der Karibik.	Barbados ______ is in the Caribbean.
2. Das Leben auf Barbados war früher brutal.	Life on Barbados was brutal ______ in the past.
3. 	There were pirates who kept their prisoners ______ on their ships.
4. Sie ließen die Gefangenen auf dem Fußboden der Kabine allein.	They left the prisoners alone ______ on the floor ______ of the cabin ______.
5. Das war eine schreckliche Strafe.	This was a terrible punishment ______.
6. Die Gefangenen riefen um Hilfe.	The prisoners cried ______ for help.
7. Aber es gab keine Reaktion. Die Tür öffnete sich nicht.	But there was no reaction ______. The door did not open ______.

17 Put a circle around the odd one out and write it in German.

1. workers • students • (prisoners) • teachers Gefangene
2. (cry) • run • walk • jump weinen; schreien; rufen
3. polite • nice • friendly • (brutal) brutal
4. table • bed • (floor) • chair Fußboden

18 Put in the right words.

although | Barbados | brutal | cabin | cried | prisoners | punishment | reaction

1. There was a ship in the Caribbean near Barbados ______.
2. Some brutal ______ pirates saw the ship. They wanted to take prisoners ______.
3. The passengers were afraid of the pirates' punishment ______.
4. Some of the women tried to hide in the cabin ______.
5. Although ______ they cried ______ for help, there was no reaction ______.

What's the word?

1. 	My neighbour had an old cannon ______ in the attic.
2. Sie zeigte in den Himmel.	It was pointing ______ at the sky ______.
3. Eines Tages drehte er sie herum.	One day he turned ______ it around ______.
4. Ich erkannte die Gefahr: Die Kanone zeigte jetzt auf unser Haus.	I recognised ______ the danger. The cannon was now pointing at our house.
5. Ich hatte große Angst.	I was terrified ______.
6. Ich musste mir etwas einfallen lassen.	I had to think of ______ something.
7. Mein Nachbar fuhr damit fort, seine Kanone immer wieder herumzudrehen.	My neighbour continued ______ to turn his cannon around again and again.
8. Eines Tages kam eine Krankenschwester und nahm ihn mit. Manchmal denke ich, er hatte Glück, dass jemand kam und sich um ihn kümmerte.	One day a nurse came and took him with her. Sometimes I think he was lucky ______ someone came and took care of him.

19 Put in the right words.

around | away | in | of | of | out

1. turn around
2. think of
3. take one's breath away
4. break out
5. terrified of
6. fit in

20 Put in the right words.

cannons | crying | lucky | pirates | prisoner | punishment | recognise | sky | terrified | think of

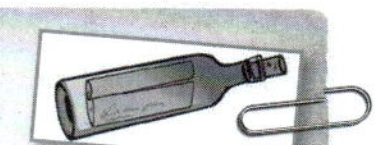

Dear friend,

Please help me! I'm a prisoner ______ in the Caribbean. Some pirates ______ have taken me away from my ship. I am terrified ______ because they always point at the cannons ______. I think this will be their punishment ______. I can't think of ______ a way to escape. I'm crying ______ for help, but only the sky ______ can hear me. If I am lucky ______, another ship will recognise ______ the pirate ship and help me.

Captain Henry

What's the word?

1. Von meinen Eltern habe ich gelernt, kein Geld zu verschwenden.	I learned from my parents not to waste ______ money.
2. Sie sagten, Reichtum kommt durch harte Arbeit.	They said wealth ______ comes with hard work.
3. Sie erwarteten Engagement von mir und anderen.	They expected commitment ______ from me and others.
4. Aber sie übernahmen auch Verantwortung für arme Leute.	But they also took responsibility ______ for poor people.
5. Sie zeigten Solidarität und halfen ihnen, einen Job zu finden.	They showed solidarity ______ and helped them to find a job.

21 Complete the words.

-ility | -ing | -ment | -ment | -ship | -tion | -ty | -ty

1. solidarity
2. responsibility
3. punishment
4. reaction
5. commitment
6. honesty
7. nursing
8. friendship

22 Complete the crossword.

						1		2		3			4	
								W		G				
						C		A		A			C	
						A	5 ▸	S	K	Y			O	
						N		T					M	
		6 ▸ 7 ▾	T	H	U	N	D	E	R				M	
		W				O							I	
8 ▸	R	E	S	P	O	N	S	I	B	I	L	I	T	Y
		A											M	
9 ▸	A	L	T	H	O	U	G	H					E	
		T											N	
		H					10 ▸	H	O	N	E	S	T	Y

Down ▾:

1. something that was used on ships for fighting
2. Don't … food!
3. When men love other men, they are …
4. If you really want this job, you have to show …
7. a lot of money

Across ▸:

5. The stars are in the …
6. … and lightning
8. adjective = responsible noun = …
9. English for *obwohl*
10. adjective = honest noun = …

What's the word?

1. Die Tür flog auf.	The door flew open ______.
2. Es war einer der Piraten. Er hatte einen bösen Ausdruck im Gesicht.	It was one of the pirates. He had an evil ______ look ______ on his face.
3. Die junge Gefangene wollte ihn nicht ansehen. Sie schaute stattdessen durch das Bullauge. Sie wartete auf Hilfe.	The young prisoner did not want to look at him. She looked through the porthole ______ instead. She was waiting for help.
4. Sie hatte Angst und dachte, der Pirat würde sie erschießen.	She was afraid and thought the pirate would shoot ______ her.
5. Der Pirat war amüsiert.	The pirate was amused ______.
6. Es war das Jahr 1625. Damals gab es in der Karibik viele Piraten. Sie nahmen gern britische Gefangene.	It was 1625. There were a lot of pirates in the Caribbean at that time ______. They liked to take British prisoners.

23 Look at the pictures and write the words.

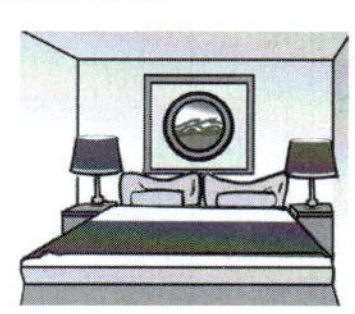

1. evil look
2. porthole
3. amused

24 Make sentences. Put the words in the right order.

1. door • Suddenly • open • and • mother • the • flew • room. • my • entered • the
   Suddenly the door flew open and my mother entered the room.
2. wasn't • look. • and • I • gave • amused • evil • her • an
   I wasn't amused and gave her an evil look.
3. didn't • know • I • time. • would • become • a • I • musician • famous • at • that
   I didn't know I would become a famous musician at that time.
4. can • sharks • see • the • through • You • porthole. • the
   You can see the sharks through the porthole.

What's the word?

1. Der Pirat nahm die Gefangene mit aufs Schiffsdeck. — The pirate took the prisoner up to the deck.
2. Sie fiel auf den Boden. Sie brauchte einen Moment, bis sie wieder aufstehen konnte. — She fell on the floor. It took her a moment to get up again.
3. Sie konnte einen Schuss hören. — She could hear a shot.
4. Ein anderer Pirat feuerte weitere Schüsse in die Luft ab. — Another pirate fired more shots into the air.
5. Da wusste sie, sie würde über eine Schiffsplanke ins Wasser getrieben werden. — That was when she knew she would have to walk the plank.

25 Look at the pictures and write the words.

1. fire a shot
2. deck
3. walk the plank

26 Put a circle around the right words.

1. He took no responsibility (for • to • with) the fire in the office.
2. Sam shows great commitment (of • to • with) his work.
3. Jerry is gay. At first he was afraid he wouldn't fit (in • out • with).
4. I feel no solidarity (in • of • with) rude people.
5. She has faith (in • out • with) her friends.
6. She can always rely (of • on • for) them.
7. When you are in trouble, you have to think (from • with • of) something.
8. I was terrified (from • with • of) him (at • in • of) that time.

What's the word?

1. In Südafrika sprechen viele Menschen Englisch. — Many people speak English in South Africa.
2. Nelson Mandela war der erste schwarze Präsident. — Nelson Mandela was the first black president.
3. Der Sitz der Regierung ist in Pretoria. — The seat of government is in Pretoria.
4.  — The money from tourists and diamond mines is very important for South Africa.
5. In Südafrika kann man auf Safari gehen. — You can go on a safari in South Africa.
6. Auf einer Safari kann man wilde Tiere sehen. — On a safari you can see wild animals.
7. Viele Touristen gehen auf Safari, um Löwen zu sehen. — Many tourists go on a safari to see lions.
8. Die meisten von ihnen wollen auch Nashörner sehen. — Most of them want to see rhinos too.

1 Look at the pictures and write the words.

1. lion
2. rhino
3. South Africa

2 Make sentences. Put the words in the right order.

1. year. • next • to • South Africa • go • want • I • to
   I want to go to South Africa next year.
2. film • about • yesterday. • diamond • mine • a • a • saw • I
   I saw a film about a diamond mine yesterday.
3. Rhinos • animals. • lions • are • wild • and
   Rhinos and lions are wild animals.
4. has • country • capitals. • The • three
   The country has three capitals.

What's the word?

1. Der bekannteste Nationalpark ist der Kruger-Nationalpark. — The most famous national park is Kruger National Park.
2. Er ist ein Naturreservat, in dem die Menschen Tiere, Pflanzen und Landschaft schützen. — It is a nature reserve where people protect plants, animals and the landscape.
3. Südafrikaner lieben ihr Land und dessen Tiere. — South Africans love their country and its animals.
4.  — The *Daily Sun* is one of the biggest newspapers in South Africa.
5. In den Medien kann man jeden Tag Berichte über die Tierwelt Südafrikas lesen. — You can read reports about South Africa's wildlife in the media every day.

3 Put in the right words.

national parks | newspaper | report | rhinos | safari

The Cape Town Observer
Cape Town's oldest newspaper

On a safari
See the last rhinos in our national parks

A report by Jan de Mool

4 Match the sentence parts.

1. South Africa's population is
2. South Africans are proud
3. South Africa is famous
4. There are many nature reserves
5. Newspapers report about

a) of their first black president, Nelson Mandela.
b) for its national parks.
c) the government, sports and wildlife.
d) mostly African.
e) to protect animals.

What's the word?

1. Die Niederländer kamen vor etwa 400 Jahren nach Südafrika. — The Dutch came to South Africa about 400 years ago.
2. Apartheid ist ein trauriger Teil der Geschichte Südafrikas. — Apartheid is a sad part of South African history.
3.  — Apartheid separated black and white people.
4. Nelson Mandela wollte ein neues Südafrika gründen. — Nelson Mandela wanted to build a new South Africa.
5. Er wollte einen Staat gründen, in dem Schwarze und Weiße in Frieden zusammenleben können. — He wanted to build a nation in which black and white people could live together in peace.

5 Match the words and their meanings.

1. apartheid
2. media
3. build
4. nation
5. separate

a) country
b) make or start something
c) a system that separated black and white people
d) newspapers, magazines, TV and the internet
e) put into two groups

6 Put in the right words.

apartheid | media | nations | separated | the Dutch

1. Apartheid ended in 1994.
2. In many countries the media reported about the end of apartheid.
3. Now black and white people are not separated by law any more.
4. I hope that one day all nations will live together in peace.
5. The Dutch built a colony in South Africa 400 years ago.

What's the word?

1. Townships sind sehr arme Wohngegenden. — Townships are very poor areas.
2. Reiche Leute leben oft in bewachten Wohnanlagen mit hoher Sicherheit. — Rich people often live in gated communities with high security.
3. Während der Apartheid gab es Krieg. — There was a war during apartheid.
4. Südafrika ist jetzt ein demokratisches Land. — Now South Africa is a democratic country.
5.  — People can vote for the president.
6. Die Verfassung gibt dem Staat, der Regierung und den Menschen Regeln. — The constitution gives rules to the country, the government and the people.
7. Alle fünf Jahre gibt es Präsidentschaftswahlen. — There are elections for president every five years.

7 Choose the right word.

constitution | democratic | townships | separate | vote | war

1. nation • rules • constitution
2. city • gated communities • townships
3. president • elections • vote
4. good • free • democratic
5. fight • soldier • war
6. apartheid • black people • separate

8 Complete the two mind maps.

constitution | democratic | election | internet | newspaper | report | TV | vote

government: constitution, election, vote, democratic

media: internet, report, newspaper, TV

What's the word?

1. In Südafrika müssen Familien für Privatschulen zahlen. — In South Africa families have to pay for private schools.
2. Viele arme Kinder brechen die Schule ab und versuchen, Arbeit zu finden. — Many poor children drop out of school and try to find work.
3. Ihre Eltern denken nicht an die Folgen. — Their parents don't think of the consequences.
4. Einige Kinder sind Opfer einer schlechten Familiensituation. — Some children are the victims of a bad family situation.
5. Arme Familien haben oft keine Krankenversicherung. — Poor families often don't have health insurance.
6. Reiche Kinder können auf Privatschulen gehen. Sie sind gut ausgebildet. — Rich children can go to private schools. They are well-educated.
7. Arme Kinder gehen stattdessen auf öffentliche Schulen. — Poor children go to state schools instead.

9 What are they saying? Complete the sentences.

consequences | dropped out of | health insurance | private school | state school | well-educated

1 My parents are poor so I had to go to a state school. But I dropped out of school. I didn't think of the consequences at the time.

2 My parents are well-educated and earn a lot of money. I can go to a private school. My parents also have good health insurance.

10 Put a circle around the right words.

1. Poor children often (drop out of • separate from) school to earn money for the family.
2. They usually don't get skilled jobs. They are the (elections • victims) of the system.
3. Rich families often live in gated communities because they want (consequences • security).
4. Their children usually are (democratic • well-educated), get better jobs and earn more money.

What's the word?

1. Leute, die zur Mittelschicht gehören, schicken ihre Kinder auf öffentliche Schulen. — People who are middle class send their children to state schools.
2. Viele Leute denken, dass es nicht gerecht ist, dass man für eine gute Bildung zahlen muss. — Many people think it isn't fair that you have to pay for a good education.
3. Kinder, die auf Privatschulen gehen, sind privilegiert. — Children who can go to private schools are privileged.
4. Ich denke, alle Kinder sollten im Leben die gleichen Chancen haben. — I think all children should have equal opportunities in life.
5. Kinder in armen Gegenden fühlen sich oft nicht sicher. — Children in poor areas often don't feel secure.
6. Ihre Situation macht sie zu Außenseitern der Gesellschaft. — Their situation often makes them outcasts in society.

11 Match the opposites. ↔

1. outcast
2. be privileged
3. fair
4. equal
5. feel secure

a) not OK
b) not the same
c) have few opportunities
d) be afraid
e) part of a group

12 Make sentences. Put the words in the right order.

1. who • People • car • often • have • a • middle-class • and • house. • are • a
   People who are middle-class often have a car and a house.
2. children • Germany • are • Many • privileged. • in
   Many children in Germany are privileged.
3. school. • feels • an • Lefa • outcast • at • like
   Lefa feels like an outcast at school.
4. equal • are • All • law. • people • under • the
   All people are equal under the law.

What's the word?

1. Mein Vater arbeitet auf dem Bau. Letzte Woche hat er einen Unfall beobachtet. — My father works in construction. He saw an accident last week.
2. 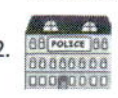 — So he wrote a letter to the police station.
3. Er begann mit „Sehr geehrte Damen und Herren, …". — He started the letter with 'Dear Sir or Madam,'.
4. Er schrieb, was er beobachtet hatte, und beendete den Brief mit „Mit freundlichen Grüßen" und seinem Namen. — He wrote about what he had seen and ended the letter with 'Yours faithfully,' and his name.
5. Papa erzählte mir, dass er immer noch Rückblenden von einem Unfall hat, den er als Jugendlicher hatte. Ich glaube, deshalb wollte er nicht aufs Polizeirevier gehen. — Dad told me that he still has flashbacks of an accident he had as a teenager. I think that is why he didn't want to go to the police station.

13 Match the sentences with the pictures.

Tsire cannot play football for two months. | The driver was taken to the police station. | My cousin Tsire was the victim of an accident. | It is still not clear what caused the accident. | The driver of the other car was a priviliged white man. | He has flashbacks about the accident.

1. My cousin Tsire was the victim of an accident.

2. The driver of the other car was a privileged white man.

3. It is still not clear what caused the accident.

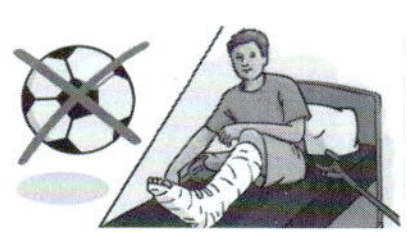

4. Tsire cannot play football for two months.

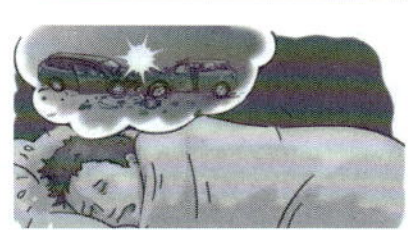

5. He has flashbacks about the accident.

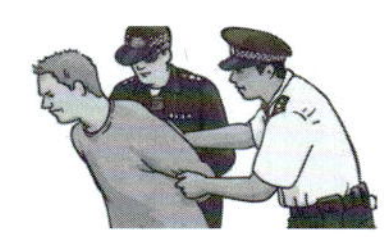

6. The driver was taken to the police station.

What's the word?

1. Mein Bruder hatte letzte Woche einen Autounfall. Dieser hat ihn zu Tode erschreckt. — My brother had a car accident last week. It frightened the hell out of him.
2. Jetzt hat er manchmal Albträume. — Now he has nightmares sometimes.
3. Er kann nicht glauben, dass irgendein Idiot ein Leben in einer Sekunde zerstören kann. — He can't believe someone stupid could ruin a life in one second.
4. Er fühlt sich schuldig, weil der Fahrer des Autos hinter ihm auch verletzt wurde. — He feels guilty because the driver of the car behind him got hurt too.
5. Wir sind arm und daher bekommt er keine Behandlung gegen seine Albträume. — We are poor so he doesn't get any treatment for his nightmares.
6. Wir haben weder eine Krankenversicherung noch genug Geld, um selbst für die Behandlung zu zahlen. — We have neither health insurance nor enough money to pay for the treatment ourselves.

14 Put in the right words.

drop out of · frightened the hell out of · guilty · health insurance · neither ... nor · nightmares · Police Station · Sir or Madam · treatment · Yours faithfully

Dear Sir or Madam,

I am writing to you because my husband had a car accident near Durban Police Station. He was not guilty. I saw the accident. The noise frightened the hell out of me. I have nightmares now. My husband cannot pay for the treatment he needs because he can neither work nor get health insurance. We have five children and we cannot pay for the flat and food for all of us, so the oldest will have to drop out of school. Can you please help us?

Yours faithfully,

Sikabe Mbongo

What's the word?

1. In manchen Nationalparks gibt es Sandebenen. — In some national parks there are sand plains.
2. Um die Nationalparks wurden Zäune errichtet. — Fences were built around the national parks.
3. Einige Parks sind auch Wüsten. — Some parks are deserts too.
4. Sümpfe können gefährlich sein, weil das Land dort nass ist. — Marshes can be dangerous because the land is wet there.
5. Auch Gebirge können Teil eines Naturreservats sein. — Mountain ranges can be part of a nature reserve too.
6. Ranger begannen ihre Arbeit, als der Kruger-Nationalpark 1927 eröffnete. — Rangers started working when Kruger National Park opened in 1927.
7. Seitdem beschützen sie die Tiere im Park. — They have protected the animals in the park ever since.
8. Ihr Ziel ist es, Tiere wie Elefanten und Nashörner zu erhalten. — Their goal is to conserve animals like elephants and rhinos.
9. Der Kruger-Nationalpark wurde nach Präsident Kruger benannt, der von 1883 bis 1900 Präsident von Südafrika war. — Kruger Park was named after President Kruger, who was president of South Africa from 1883 to 1900.

15 Look at the pictures and write the words.

1. mountain range

2. marsh

3. plain

4. ranger

5. desert

6. fence

What's the word?

1. Natur und Tiere sind sehr wichtig für den Tourismus in Südafrika. — Nature and animals are very important for South African tourism.
2. Besucher müssen einen Führer anheuern. Sie dürfen nicht allein gehen. — Visitors must hire a guide. They mustn't go on their own.
3. Sie dürfen auch ihren Abfall nicht im Park zurücklassen. — They also mustn't leave their waste in the park.
4. Die meisten Touristen möchten die Tiere beobachten. Aber manche wollen sie jagen. — Most tourists want to watch the animals. But some want to hunt them.
5. Manche Jäger jagen Elefanten wegen ihres Elfenbeins, was nicht erlaubt ist. — Some hunt elephants for their ivory, which is not allowed.
6. Die Regierung regelt die Zahl der Jäger und Touristen. — The government regulates the number of hunters and tourists.
7.  — That is why the numbers of leopards are going up again.
8. Büffel können auch gejagt werden. — Buffaloes can be hunted too.
9. Elefanten, Leoparden, Nashörner und Büffel sind Wild. — Elephants, leopards, rhinos and buffaloes are game.

16 Look at the pictures and write the words.

1. buffalo

2. ivory

3. game

17 Put a circle around the right words.

1. Elephants, buffaloes and rhinos are (game · play).
2. There are (leopards · kangaroos) in South Africa too.
3. National parks are very important for (tourism · factories).
4. Hunters are not allowed to (hire · hunt) for ivory.
5. Rules (conserve · regulate) what tourists can and can't do in the parks.

What's the word?

1. Die Ranger behandeln die Tiere mit Respekt. — Rangers treat the animals with respect.
2. Jedes Lebewesen verdient Respekt. — Every creature deserves respect.
3. Wenn man sieht, dass ein Tier nicht gut behandelt wird, sollte man eingreifen. — If you see that an animal is not treated well, you should take action.
4. Jagen, das gegen das Gesetz verstößt, nennt man Wilderei. — Hunting that is against the law is called poaching.
5. In der letzten Ausgabe der Zeitschrift „Wild Africa" war ein Bericht über Wilderei. — There was a report about poaching in the latest edition of the *Wild Africa* magazine.
6. Ich habe gelesen, dass die neue Regierung jetzt handelt und die Zeit für Wilderei jetzt abgelaufen ist. — I read that the new government is taking action and that time for poaching is up.

18 Put a circle around the odd one out and write it in German.

1. good · respect · fair · equal — Respekt
2. sit · take action · wait · sleep — eingreifen; handeln
3. buffalo · rhino · treat · leopard — behandeln
4. ranger · nurse · hunter · tourism — Tourismus

19 Match the sentence parts.

1. Have you read the latest
2. There was a report
3. Poaching is
4. The government has taken
5. I think the time
6. Animals deserve

a) against the law.
b) to be treated with respect.
c) edition of the *Wild Africa* magazine?
d) for hunters is up.
e) action to protect wild animals.
f) on poaching.

What's the word?

1. Ich hatte die Grundschule im Sommer beendet und würde bald auf die Johannesburger Stadtschule gehen.	I had finished primary school ______ in the summer and would soon start at Johannesburg City School.
2. Im September waren die Ferien vorbei und das neue Schuljahr begann.	In September the holidays were over ______ and the new school year began ______.
3. In der Schule gab es einen richtigen Spielplatz, nicht nur trockenen Erdboden zum Spielen.	There was a real playground at the school, not just some dry ground ______ to play on.
4. Sie hatten auch einen großen Sportplatz.	They also had a large playing field ______.
5. Er war besser als der an meiner alten Schule, wo ich oft hingefallen bin und mir am Hintern wehgetan habe.	It was better than the one at my old school, where I had often fallen and hurt my bottom ______.
6. Mein Klassenlehrer war ein Schwarzer.	My class teacher was a black person ______.
7. An seinem ersten Tag an der Schule waren draußen vor dem Schulgebäude Demonstranten.	On his first day at the school there were protesters ______ outside the school building.
8. Ich mag es nicht, wenn Leute gegen Schwarze protestieren, nur weil sie Schwarze sind.	I don't like it when people protest ______ against black people just because they are black.
9. Ich hoffe, unser Lehrer muss sich nicht allein um diese Leute kümmern.	I hope our teacher doesn't have to deal with ______ those people alone.

20 Look at the pictures and complete the sentences.

1. The year is over ______.

2. There are many protesters ______ in the streets today.

3. My little sister goes to primary school ______.

4. Zoe is my best friend. She's black ______.

5. My Saturday job begins ______ in October.

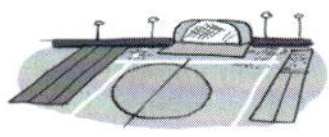

6. The playing field ______ of our school is quite large.

What's the word?

1. Mein Klassenlehrer ist auch der Schulleiter meiner neuen Schule.	My class teacher also is the headteacher ______ of my new school.
2. Er warnte uns, unsere Smartphones während des Unterrichts nicht zu benutzen.	He warned ______ us not to use our smartphones during class.
3. 	We were just talking about my favourite animals, baboons ______.
4. Ein Junge versuchte, sein Telefon unter dem Tisch zu benutzen.	One boy tried ______ to use his phone under the desk.
5. Der Lehrer sah ihn an und fragte: „Benutzt irgendjemand gerade sein Telefon?"	The teacher looked in his direction and asked, "Is anyone ______ using his or her phone at the moment?"
6. Er meinte es ernst. Er scherzte nicht.	He was serious. He wasn't joking ______.
7. Aber während der Pausen lässt er uns in Ruhe.	But he leaves us alone ______ during the breaks.
8. Nach der letzten Klassenarbeit schaute er traurig, schüttelte den Kopf und sagte: „Ihr habt alle ziemlich schlecht abgeschnitten."	After the last class test he looked sad, shook his head ______ and said, "All of you did pretty badly."
9. 	But then he smiled ______. He was only joking.

21 Put in the right words.

Jenny's blog – the pink cat

Hi there. How is it going?

Holiday time is up ______ and I'm back at school ☹. My older brother's friend Kagiso visited us during the holidays. They went to primary school ______ together. My father was the headteacher ______ there. Kagiso was the first black ______ boy at Jan's school. Some parents protested ______ outside the school building and their kids tried ______ to push Kagiso. But Dad warned ______ them to leave him alone ______. Kagiso is really good at rugby and he's cool. He joked ______ with me all the time. When he left, he smiled ______ at me … 😊

black
joked
headteacher
up
primary school
smiled
leave him alone
protested
tried
warned

What's the word?

1. Eltern sind unverantwortlich, wenn sie sich nicht um ihre Kinder kümmern.	Parents are irresponsible ______ if they don't care for their children.
2. Einige arme Familien sind abhängig von dem Geld, das ihre Kinder verdienen.	Some poor families are dependent ______ on the money their children earn.
3. Arme Kinder haben oft weniger Chancen als reiche Kinder. Sie sind benachteiligt.	Poor children often don't have as many chances as rich kids. They are underprivileged ______.
4. 	Some of them work for rich people. They look after their gardens and ponds ______.
5. Mein Nachbar hat eine eigene Quelle in seinem Garten.	My neighbour has his own spring ______ in his garden.
6. Die reichen Leute leben in den Hügeln, aber die meisten armen Familien wohnen in Townships unten im Tal.	The rich people live in the hills, but most poor families live in townships down in the valley ______.
7. Der Hauptteil unserer Stadt liegt im Tal.	The main ______ part of our town is in the valley.
8. 	Huge cactuses ______ grow along the main road.

22 Look at the pictures and complete the sentences.

1. A driver is irresponsible ______ when he drinks and drives.

2. His parents are poor and he is underprivileged ______.

3. The baby is dependent ______ on its mother.

23 Match the opposites. ⟷

1. responsible	a) end
2. dependent	b) underprivileged
3. hill	c) agree
4. privileged	d) irresponsible
5. protest	e) independent
6. begin	f) valley

What's the word?

1. Letztes Jahr wechselten Mama und Papa sich ab, mich von der Schule abzuholen.	Last year Mum and Dad took turns ______ picking me up from school.
2. 	Mum ironed ______ for rich families and Dad looked after their gardens.
3. Die beiden arbeiteten sehr hart.	The two of them ______ worked very hard.
4. Eine Familie, die van Betuws, haben einen Rasensprenger, um ihren Garten schön und grün zu halten.	One family, the van Betuws, have a sprinkler ______ to keep their garden nice and green.
5. Ich war mit Papa gern dort und schnitt lustige Grimassen unter dem Rasensprenger.	I liked to be there with Dad and made funny faces ______ under the sprinkler.
6. Die van Betuws hatten auch einen kleinen Hund. Manchmal versuchte er, Leute anzugreifen, und rannte wie ein Wilder umher.	The van Betuws also had a little dog. Sometimes it tried to attack people and ran around like a savage ______.
7. Aber Papa hat einen Fehler gemacht und jetzt ist er lebenslang im Gefängnis.	But Dad did something wrong and now he is in prison for life ______.
8. 	This is why I pray ______ for him and our family every night.

24 Put a circle around the right words.

1. My best friend Malik and his father go to church every Sunday to (talk • pray).
2. Jane made funny (faces • feet) at me.
3. I have two older brothers. The (two • main) of them are good at rugby.
4. They are taking (time • turns) helping Dad in the garden.
5. Nelson Mandela was put in prison (for life • always) because he wanted to end apartheid.

25 Complete the words.

A A E E E E E E E I I I I I I
O O O U U

1. iron
2. take turns
3. for life
4. pray
5. irresponsible
6. underprivileged

What's the word?

1.  — We went to Addo Elephant National Park at the beginning of the *New Year*.
2. Als wir zu den Tieren gingen, hielt Mama meine Hand richtig fest. — When we walked to the animals, Mum held my hand really *tight*.
3. Aber sie konnte mich nicht davon abhalten, vor den großen Tieren Angst zu haben. — But she couldn't *stop me from* being afraid of the big animals.
4. Ein Ranger wandte sich mir zu und fragte: „Möchtest du den kleinen Elefanten füttern?" — A ranger *turned to me* and asked, "Do you want to feed the little elephant?"
5. Ich schüttelte den Kopf und wurde rot. — I shook my head and *went red*.
6. Er war wirklich nett und sagte: „Hab' keine Angst. Mach es schrittweise." — He was really nice and said, "Don't be afraid. Take it *one step at a time*."
7. Also holte ich tief Luft und streckte langsam meine Hand aus. — So I *took a deep breath* and slowly held out my hand.

26 Look at the pictures and complete the sentences.

1. I was nervous, but my friend held my hand very *tight*.

2. When the teacher asked Linda if she knew the answer, she *went red*.

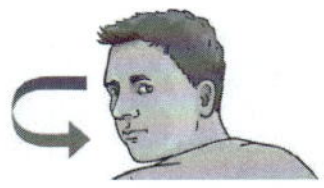
3. When I called Sam, he *turned to me*.

27 Complete the sentences.

at | for | from | of | on | to | with

1. The boys *on* the bus turned *to* me and smiled.
2. The two *of* them looked really cool.
3. It's always good to take one step *at* a time.
4. Teachers have to deal *with* naughty kids.
5. My friends stopped me *from* making a big mistake.
6. My neighbour is in prison *for* life because he started a shooting and killed someone.

What's the word?

1. China ist ein faszinierendes Land. — *China* is a fascinating country.
2. Dort eröffnen jede Woche riesige neue Einkaufszentren. — Huge new *malls* open there every week.
3. Aber es gibt auch Straßenmärkte mit Essensständen und Wahrsagern. — But there are also street markets with food stalls and *fortune tellers*.
4. Viele Kunden fahren mit dem Auto in die Einkaufszentren. Das verursacht Luftverschmutzung. — Many customers drive to the malls. This causes air *pollution*.
5. Wenn viel Verschmutzung in der Luft ist, sieht der Himmel grau aus. Man nennt das Smog. — If there is a lot of air pollution, the sky looks grey. People call it *smog*.
6. Smog verursacht Gesundheitsprobleme für die Menschen in großen Städten wie Hongkong. — Smog causes *health* problems for people in big cities like Hong Kong.
7. Obwohl Hongkong Verschmutzungsprobleme hat, ist es eine unglaubliche Stadt. Sie ist eine Mischung aus Osten und Westen. — Although Hong Kong has pollution problems, it's an amazing city. It's a *mixture* of East and West.

1 Look at the pictures and write the words.

1. *fortune teller*

2. *mall*

3. *China*

2 Find the words. Write them in English and German.

pollution – Verschmutzung
smog – Smog
health – Gesundheit-; gesundheitlich
China – China
mall – Einkaufszentrum
mixture – Mischung

What's the word?

1. Leute, die beim Einkaufen immer neue Plastiktüten verwenden, verursachen immer mehr Verschmutzung. — People who use new plastic bags every time they go shopping *create* more pollution.
2. Wir sollten die Zahl der Plastiktüten, die wir verwenden, reduzieren. — We should try to *reduce* the number of plastic bags we use.
3.  — Some types of plastic can be *recycled*.
4. Smog ist der Grund, warum die Regierung versucht, die Zahl der Autos in den belebten Teilen der Stadt zu reduzieren. — Smog is why the government tries to reduce the number of cars in the *busy* parts of the city.
5. Jeden Tag gibt es viele Medienberichte über Smog. — There are a lot of *media* reports about smog every day.

3 Put in the right words.

busiest | China | fortune tellers | health | malls
media | mixture | reduce | recycle | pollution | smog

E-MAIL

Dear Mum and Dad,
Hong Kong is really fascinating! It's a *mixture* of East and West. It's the *busiest* city in China. It became part of *China* in 1997, but it has a special status. There are so many shops, markets and *malls*. They sell clothes, smartphones and Chinese food. You can go shopping day and night. But Hong Kong is also famous for its busy *media* industry.
But because of all the people, the city has a problem with *pollution* and smog. The people here try to *reduce* waste and to *recycle* as much as they can. But the *smog* is really bad. Sometimes the sky is so grey you can't see the sun. Smog can cause *health* problems.
Let's hope that the *fortune tellers* who say the air will be better in 2025 are right. ☺
Love,
Danny

What's the word?

1. Wie viele Punkte würdest du China für seine Aktivitäten zur Reduzierung von Verschmutzung geben? — How many *points* would you give China for its activities to reduce pollution?
2. 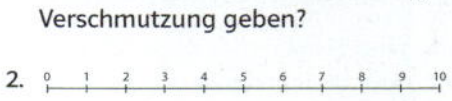 — On a *scale* of one to ten I would give it a three.

3. Die Europäer versuchen, die Verschmutzung auf andere Art und Weise zu verringern. — Europeans try to reduce pollution in a *different* way.
4. Aber der Smog in der Stuttgarter oder Hamburger Innenstadt ist auch wirklich schlimm. — But the smog in *downtown* Stuttgart or Hamburg is really bad too.
5. Die Regierung setzt die Industrie unter Druck, etwas daran zu ändern. — The government has put industries under *pressure* to change something.

4 Look at the pictures and complete the sentences.

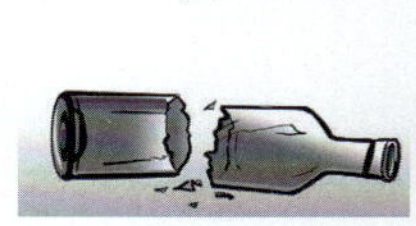
1. The bottle was under *pressure*. Now it's broken.

2. The air *downtown* is really bad.

3. He got ten *points* in the test.

5 Find eight words. (↓ and →) Write them in English and German.

E	F	N	D	C	M	E	D	I	A	O
A	N	S	D	R	C	P	O	I	N	T
K	I	B	B	E	X	G	W	Y	P	H
B	R	I	G	A	Q	C	N	F	R	Q
U	J	I	C	T	W	F	T	L	E	D
S	C	A	L	E	S	V	O	Q	S	E
Y	H	A	F	T	F	X	W	A	S	C
D	I	F	F	E	R	E	N	T	U	B
K	O	P	C	U	F	W	Q	I	R	L
R	I	J	L	O	P	A	S	D	E	L

media – Medien-
point – Punkt
scale – Skala; Maßstab; Ausmaß
different – unterschiedlich; verschieden; anders
busy – rege; belebt; aktiv
create – verursachen; ausmachen
downtown – Innenstadt; im Stadtzentrum
pressure – Druck

What's the word?

1. Hast du die neuesten Nachrichten auf Jenny Wongs Blog gelesen? — Have you read the latest news on Jenny Wong's blog?
2. Jenny ist Expertin für Mode. Sie durchstöbert jeden Tag Geschäfte und Märkte. — Jenny is an expert on fashion. She browses shops and markets every day.
3. 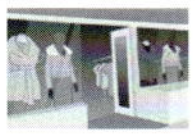 — Last week she saw a cool bag in a shop window and bought it.
4. Sie schreibt in ihrem Blog auch, wie man mit Mode Geld verdienen kann. — In her blog she also writes about how to make money with fashion.
5. Sie postet immer ein Bild, wenn sie brandneue Kleidung gekauft hat. — She always posts a picture when she has bought brand-new clothes.

6 Put in the right words.

brand-new · browse · downtown · latest · make money · pressure · scale · shop windows

Miss Fashion's trendy blog

Hi everyone!
Can you believe it? I finally found that brand-new bag in Eric Wu's shop. On a scale of one to ten I would give it a nine. I was browsing shop windows in Cheung Sha Wan Road in downtown Hong Kong when I suddenly saw it! It's so hard to find the latest clothes if you don't browse the shops every day. But don't put yourself under pressure. Shopping must be fun! Next time I'll tell you how to make money by recycling old clothes.
CU soon,
Miss Fashion

What's the word?

1. Normalerweise verkauft Miss Fashion ihre Kleidung wieder, nachdem sie sie nur einmal getragen hat. Dazu hebt sie immer den Originalkarton auf. — Usually Miss Fashion resells her clothes after wearing them only once. That's why she always keeps the original box.
2. Sie liebt den Handel mit Taschen genauso, wie sie zu besitzen. — She loves trading bags as much as owning them.
3.  — And she sometimes swaps bags with her friends.
4. Sie schreibt auch darüber, wie man coole gebrauchte Kleidung findet. — She also writes about finding cool second-hand clothes.
5. Einige Second-Hand-Läden verkaufen Dinge, die Leute gespendet haben, und geben das Geld dann armen Kindern. — Some second-hand shops sell things that people donated and then give the money to poor children.
6. Man kann seine Stadt kontaktieren, um mehr über das Wiederverkaufen, Tauschen und Spenden von Dingen zu erfahren. — You can contact your town to learn more about reselling, swapping or donating things.
7. Wenn man drei Taschen bei Miss Fashion kauft, erhält man 10 % Rabatt. — If you buy three bags from Miss Fashion, you will get a 10% discount.

7 Make sentences. Put the words in the right order.

1. buys • the • fashion. • My • latest • always • sister
   My sister always buys the latest fashion.
2. best • First • swapped • her • with • she • Jenny. • friend • clothes
   First she swapped clothes with her best friend Jenny.
3. things • reselling • began • money. • she • make • Then • to
   Then she began reselling things to make money.
4. books • her • to • help • children. • old • clothes • she • and • poor • Sometimes • donates
   Sometimes she donates her old books and clothes to help poor children.

8 Complete the words.

A A A A E E E E I I I O O O O U

1. original
2. discount
3. resell
4. donate
5. second-hand
6. contact

What's the word?

1. Hast du schon mal von den „Sneakerheads" gehört? — Have you ever heard about 'sneakerheads'?
2. Ein Sneakerhead kaufte ein Paar Sneaker für 5.000 Hongkong-Dollar. Das sind mehr als 500 Euro. — One sneakerhead bought a pair of sneakers for 5,000 Hong Kong dollars. That's more than 500 euros.
3. Er ist fast ausgeflippt, als er sein Lieblingspaar Goldsneaker gefunden hat. — He almost went crazy when he found his favourite pair of golden sneakers.
4. Manche Sneakerheads kampieren sogar draußen vor den Läden, um die neuesten und verrücktesten Sneaker zu bekommen. — Some sneakerheads even camp outside the shops to get the latest and craziest sneakers.
5. Henry Fong behauptet, dass er mehr als 1.000 Paar Sneaker besitzt. — Henry Fong claims to own more than 1,000 pairs of sneakers.
6. Ich würde nie mein ganzes Taschengeld für Sneaker ausgeben. — I would never spend all my pocket money on sneakers.
7. Ich habe meine letzten Sneaker mehr als ein Jahr lang jeden Tag getragen. — I wore my last sneakers every day for more than a year.
8. Ich vermute, dass Sneakerheads wie Henry echt reich sind. Die Armen könnten nicht einmal ein Paar teure Sneaker kaufen. — I guess sneakerheads like Henry are really rich. The poor can't even buy one pair of expensive sneakers.

9 Look at the pictures and write the words.

1. sneakers

2. the poor

3. a pair of jeans

4. go crazy

5. pocket money

6. camp

What's the word?

1. Es gibt viele Wege, wie man die Luftverschmutzung verbessern kann. — There are many ways to improve air pollution.
2. Jimmy Jang ist Talkmaster von Hongkongs berühmtester Radioshow „Grüneres Hongkong". — Jimmy Jang is the host of Hong Kong's most famous radio show, *Greener Hong Kong*.
3. Er spricht über Verschmutzung und erneuerbare Energie. — He talks about pollution and renewable energy.
4. Experten sagen, dass viele Kraftwerke noch immer Öl und Kohle verwenden, um Strom zu erzeugen. — Experts say that many power plants still use oil and coal to produce electricity.
5. Sie arbeiten an neuen Technologien, um saubere Energie zu erzeugen. — They are working on new technologies to produce clean energy.
6. Es gibt verschiedene Möglichkeiten, etwas gegen Luftverschmutzung zu unternehmen. — There are different options to do something about air pollution.
7.  — At the moment people wear masks to protect themselves.
8. Mit umweltfreundlichen Technologien bräuchten die Leute keine Masken mehr. — With eco-friendly technologies people wouldn't need masks any more.
9. Aber es gibt noch andere Probleme. In der Zeitung habe ich gelesen, dass Leute im Alter von 30 bis 45 den Großteil unserer Lebensmittelabfälle produzieren. — But there are other problems too. I read in the newspaper that people aged 30 to 45 produce most of our food waste.

10 Look at the pictures and write the words.

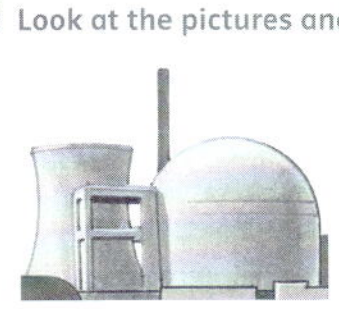
1. power plant

2. food waste

3. host

11 Put a circle around the odd one out and write it in German.

1. waste • power plant • mask • (improve) — verbessern
2. factories • cars • (eco-friendly) • planes — umweltfreundlich
3. host • (option) • nurse • plumber — Möglichkeit; Wahl; Option

What's the word?

1. Jimmy gibt auch Tipps, wie man Energie sparen kann. Er sagt, dass man einen Bewegungsmelder verwenden kann, um das Licht einzuschalten. – Jimmy gives tips on how to save energy too. He says you can use a motion sensor to turn on your lights.
2. Und man kann Sonnenkollektoren verwenden, um warmes Wasser für die Dusche oder die Badewanne zu erzeugen. – And you can use solar panels to produce hot water for your shower or bath.
3. Es gibt auch transparente Sonnenkollektoren. – There are also transparent solar panels.
4. Ein Sonnenkollektor wird aus vielen kleinen Solarzellen hergestellt. – A solar panel is made of many small solar cells.
5. Wind- und Sonnenenergie produzieren keine Abgase wie Autos. – Wind and solar energy don't produce exhaust fumes like cars.
6. Es gibt viele Entwicklungen bei den erneuerbaren Energien. – There has been a lot of development in renewable energies.
7. Chinesische Experten testen derzeit Gondeln, die die Menschen von einem Ort in der Stadt zu einem anderen bringen. – Chinese experts are testing pods that take people from one place of the city to another.
8.  – People can get on and off where they like. The pods look a bit like ski lifts.

12 Look at the pictures and complete the sentences.

1. You can see through water. It's transparent.
2. Cars produce a lot of exhaust fumes.
3. Many homes have solar panels now.

13 Put a circle around the right words.

1. Our eco-friendly car produces very few (electricity • exhaust fumes).
2. (Power plants • Solar panels) need the sun to produce energy.
3. There has been a lot of (development • energy) in new technologies since the 1980s.

What's the word?

1. Die Gondeln, über die Jimmy spricht, fahren über dem Boden. – The pods Jimmy talks about travel above the ground.
2. Du kannst zu Hause in eine Gondel einsteigen und sie setzt dich an der Schule ab. – You can get on a pod at home and it drops you off at school.
3.  – The pods have solar panels on their roof.
4. Jimmy behauptete, dass sich die Luftqualität in einigen Gegenden schon verbessert habe. – Jimmy claimed that air quality had already improved in some areas.
5.  – The pods don't travel on the ground, so grass and flowers can grow.
6. Das ist nicht nur ein positiver Effekt für die Umwelt, es sieht auch nett aus. – That's not only a positive effect for the environment, it also looks nice.
7. Jimmy hat Bilder und Diagramme über die Effekte auf seine Webseite gestellt. – Jimmy put pictures and charts about the effects on his website.
8. Die Diagramme zeigen, dass das Verschmutzungsniveau verringert werden kann, wenn wir mit Solargondeln fahren. – The charts show that pollution levels can be reduced if we travel by solar pods.

14 Match the words.

1. pollution – d) levels
2. drop – a) off
3. positive – b) effect
4. air – c) quality

a) off
b) effect
c) quality
d) levels

15 Complete the two mind maps.

eco-friendly technologies | exhaust fumes | green energy | smog | high pollution levels | power plants | recycling food waste | solar panels

good for the environment: recycling food waste, solar panels, eco-friendly technologies, green energy

bad for the environment: high pollution levels, exhaust fumes, smog, power plants

What's the word?

1. Seit der Entwicklung des Internets und der sozialen Medien gibt es viele Fragen darüber, was die Wahrheit ist. – Since the development of the internet and social media there have been a lot of questions about what the truth is.
2. Wir können online Informationen über fast alles finden, aber wir wissen nicht immer, ob sie wahr sind oder nicht. – We can find information on almost everything online, but we don't always know if it is true or not.
3. Man kann eine Menge Zeit im Internet verbringen, um die Puzzleteile zu suchen und die Wahrheit herauszufinden. – You can spend a lot of time on the internet looking for the pieces of the puzzle and find out the truth.
4. Die Presse kann Menschen beeinflussen, indem sie zum Beispiel nur Teile der Geschichte erzählt. – The press can influence people by telling only parts of the story, for example.
5. Ein Journalist muss sehr verantwortungsvoll mit den Informationen sein, die er bekommt. – A journalist must be very responsible with the information he or she gets.
6. In manchen Ländern zensiert die Regierung die Presse. – In some countries the government censors the press.
7. Sie kontrolliert die Medien und manchmal werden Journalisten verhaftet oder verschwinden. – It controls the media, and sometimes journalists get arrested or disappear.

16 Look at the pictures and write the words.

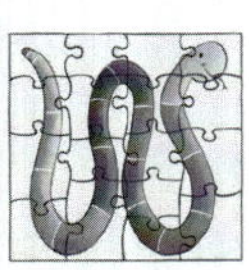

1. journalist
2. puzzle
3. press

17 Complete the words.

A A E E E E I I I O O O O O O O U U

1. information
2. truth
3. journalist
4. control
5. censor
6. development

What's the word?

1. In einer Demokratie können die Menschen in Wahlen über ihre Regierung abstimmen. – In a democracy people can vote for their government in elections.
2. Eine Demokratie schützt die Menschenrechte. Das steht in der Verfassung geschrieben. – A democracy protects human rights. This is written in the constitution.
3. Eines dieser Rechte ist die Redefreiheit. – One of those rights is the freedom of speech.
4. Das Gesetz garantiert, dass niemand wegen seiner Meinung verhaftet wird. – The law guarantees that nobody can be arrested for his or her opinion.
5. Aber es gibt Grenzen: Man muss andere Kulturen und Religionen respektieren. – But there are limits: You must respect other cultures and religions.
6. Auch die Medien sollten objektiv sein und Menschen akzeptieren, die eine andere Meinung haben. – The media should also be objective and accept people who have a different opinion.

18 Put in the right words.

censored | contact | controlled | democracy | freedom of speech | had guaranteed | human rights | information | journalist | limits | media | objective | press | truth

The Hong Kong Observer

Hong Kong Mystery

On the night of 17th March 2018 Chow Mai, a young journalist, disappeared from her home in Hong Kong. She is famous for writing the truth about human rights in China. She wrote about her opinion in many media reports. But she knew her limits and always tried to be objective. Friends told the police that Chow Mai had worked on a story about the freedom of speech. She wanted China to become a democracy. She claimed that the government controlled the press too much. The government censored some of her stories. Although it had guaranteed that she was free to write her opinion, she got some strange phone calls. Now she is gone. If you have some information, please contact our Hong Kong office at + 852 6852 1233.

What's the word?

1. Mein Vater sagte mir, dass ich kritisch mit Onlineinformationen sein solle. — My dad told me to be critical of online information.
2. Wir betrachten Menschenrechte und die Redefreiheit als selbstverständlich. — We take human rights and the freedom of speech for granted.
3. Aber man sollte immer die Quelle der Informationen überprüfen. — But you should always check the source of the information.
4. Wir haben Zugang zu so vielen Informationsquellen, dass es manchmal schwierig ist, zu sagen, was die Wahrheit ist. — We have access to so many sources of information that it is sometimes hard to tell what the truth is.
5. Einschränkungen werden die Leute nicht davon abhalten, nach der Wahrheit zu suchen. — Restrictions won't keep people from looking for the truth.
6. Einige Onlineinformationen über Hongkong sind lustig, aber nicht wahr. Ich habe gelesen, dass es eine Geschwindigkeitsgrenze für Vögel gibt, aber ich habe das nicht geglaubt. — Some online information about Hong Kong is funny but not true. I read there was a speed limit for birds, but I didn't believe it.
7. Wie viel km/h fliegen Vögel normalerweise? — How fast do those birds usually fly in mph?
8. Na ja, sie fliegen nicht viel in der Stadt. Sie sitzen lieber oben auf den Hochhäusern. — Well, they don't fly a lot in the city. They prefer sitting on top of the skyscrapers.

19 Look at the pictures and write the words.

1. speed limit
2. internet access
3. restriction

20 Put a circle around the right words.

1. People in Europe have (**access** • way) to different types of media.
2. Most people are not very (**critical** • objective) of online information.
3. In democratic societies we take human rights for (free • **granted**).
4. There is a (access • **speed limit**) for cars in towns.

What's the word?

1. Jim Jam, der einen Modeblog hat, kauft seine Sonnenbrillen in Einkaufszentren und Onlineshops. — Jim Jam, who has a fashion blog, purchases his sunglasses in malls and online shops.
2. Kleine Läden haben normalerweise nicht viele verschiedene Sonnenbrillen vorrätig. — Small shops usually don't stock a lot of different sunglasses.
3. 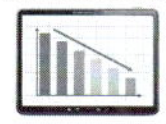 — The number of small shops has decreased because so many big online shops have opened.
4. Das erzeugt Probleme für die Leute, die in den Läden arbeiten. — This generates problems for the people working in the shops.
5. Onlineshops erhöhen manchmal am Abend ihre Preise, weil viele Leute nach der Arbeit das Internet durchstöbern. — Online shops sometimes raise their prices in the evening because many people browse the internet after work.
6. Das Onlineeinkaufen hat unser Leben verändert. — Online shopping has altered our lives.
7. Einigen Leuten da draußen ist ihr Onlineleben wichtiger als das echte Leben. — There are some people out there who think their online life is more important than real life.

21 Make sentences. Put the words in the right order.

1. people • a • purchase • Young • online. • lot
   Young people purchase a lot online.
2. cities • many • number • shops • In • the • small • decreased. • of • has
   In many cities the number of small shops has decreased.
3. downtown • stock • The • shop • sneakers. • new • doesn't • the
   The shop downtown doesn't stock the new sneakers.
4. the • like • to • Teenagers • mall • at • too. • browse • shops
   Teenagers like to browse shops at the mall too.

22 Put in the right words.

above | for | of | of | to | under

1. on top of
2. take for granted
3. freedom of speech
4. above the ground
5. under pressure
6. access to

What's the word?

1. Zeitungsverleger stellen immer mehr Informationen online. — Newspaper publishers put more and more information online.
2. Aber das macht es für Regierungen einfacher, die Medien zu kontrollieren und auf die schwarze Liste gesetzte Wörter zu finden. — But this makes it easier for governments to control the media and find blacklisted words.
3. Es ist ein Zeichen der Unterdrückung, wenn eine Regierung die Medien zensiert. — It is a sign of oppression when a government censors the media.
4. Aber es muss auch etwas Kontrolle geben, um zu gewährleisten, dass die Leute keine Gewalt verherrlichen. — But there must be some control to guarantee that people do not glorify violence.
5. In vielen Ländern findet man rechtsorientierte Kommentare im Internet. — You can find right-wing comments on the internet in many countries.
6. Jede Art von Extremismus ist schlecht. Wir sollten uns gegenseitig respektieren und andere Kulturen tolerieren. — Every type of extremism is bad. We should respect each other and tolerate different cultures.

23 Match the opposites. ↔

1. censor
2. purchase
3. oppression
4. publisher
5. increase

a) sell
b) reader
c) decrease
d) let people say and write what they want
e) freedom

24 Complete the crossword.

						1					
2 ▸				G	L	O	R	I	F	Y	
						P					
						P					
3 ▸			E	X	T	R	E	M	I	S	M
						E					
4 ▸	P	U	B	L	I	S	H	E	R		
						S					
						I					
5 ▸			D	E	M	O	C	R	A	C	Y
						N					

Down ▾:
1. when there is no freedom of speech

Across ▸:
2. say that something is really good
3. when people glorify violence and have very strong opinions
4. the person who owns a newspaper
5. Germany is a free country. It's a …

Bestandteil von
ISBN 978-3-12-547705-6
9 783125 477056